The Catch

ALSO BY MICHAEL LEESE

MARTHA MUNRO CRIME MYSTERIES
Book 1: The List
Book 2: The Trap
Book 3: The Catch

ROPER AND HOOLEY
Book 1: The Case of the Headless Billionaire
Book 2: The Case of the Missing Faces
Book 3: The Case of the Dirty Bomb
Book 4: The Case of the Exploding Shop
Book 5: The Case of the Killer Gameshow

Michael
Leese
THE CATCH

JOFFE BOOKS

Joffe Books, London
www.joffebooks.com

First published in Great Britain in 2025

Cover art by Cherie Chapman

ISBN: 978-1-80573-142-9

PROLOGUE

Southwark, London

Mexican travel guides advise against contact with the Fer de Lance, a notoriously bad-tempered snake packing venom that can virtually melt flesh. Bite victims are told to get to hospital — fast.

Which was not so easy when you were tied to a trolley inside a glass box where someone was about to release a very angry six-foot serpent.

The victim was chosen at random, just a regular twenty-something guy walking home after a rubbish date. One moment he was almost at his flat, the next he was being bundled into the back of a white van and taken to a crumbling property in Southwark, where to his horror he was tied to the trolley. Bright light shone down, exaggerating the darkness surrounding him.

Next, a seedy-looking man with a shiny forehead that reflected the light was talking to him. He spoke fast. Something about a snake — then he'd checked the restraints and disappeared into the gloom.

Then nothing. The victim tried to distract himself by thinking about his evening. His date was way out of his league. Tall, handsome and did something in the City, something that involved taking people's money and investing it wisely. Might he be interested?

He'd made an excuse and left. He might not be the smartest cookie but he knew when to walk away. Unfortunately, his decision to leave had also put him at exactly the wrong place at exactly the wrong time, as he was spotted by the two men driving around in the white van. Minutes later, he was trussed up in the back of the van and heading for Southwark to play his part in a real-life murder.

He carefully checked the restraints on the trolley. He was going nowhere. The lights dimmed and he froze at the faintest of sounds, a sort of rustling coming from the floor. He strained to try and see what it was but he couldn't make it out. What he could tell was that the noise seemed to be circling the trolley.

The lights went up and the man felt a faint vibration as something climbed up from the bottom of the trolley. He stared, eyes wide, as, inching into view, was the head of the ugliest snake he had ever seen.

The snake stopped, its tongue flickering in and out. It was looking straight at him.

Transfixed with terror, the man started begging for mercy. He might as well have asked for a large brandy at an AA meeting.

More of the snake had made it up to where the man was lying and the animal was concentrating hard on its would-be victim. As it crawled closer its tongue flicked in and out faster and faster. It reached his chest . . . and stopped.

The man was sobbing, tears running out from between his tightly closed eyes. Two other men stood outside the glass looking in. One was calm with a benign expression on his face. The other was sheet-white with a hint of green.

Inside the room, the snake was now rearing over the man as it swayed from side to side. The man with the benign expression was convinced the creature was smiling.

Almost too fast to see, the snake struck. Fangs sank into the soft flesh around the victim's neck and warm jets of venom injected into his body.

From that point, he was a dead man, although it would take a while. This was murder in slow motion.

Of the two men looking through the window, one was called Tony Green, a former high flyer and Detective Chief Inspector at Scotland Yard and now a renegade cop at the top of the most wanted list. He was a vicious sociopath who had gone to a lot of trouble to bring the snake to England because he wanted to make a point. First, he wanted it known that he was capable of killing people in a variety of deeply unpleasant and creative ways. He wanted his people to be so frightened of him that they never worried about the enemy.

Secondly, he really wanted to make an impression on his companion, which, judging by how white he had gone, was working well. They'd come back later — there really was only so long that anyone could listen to a man weeping and calling out for his mother. *Seen one, seen them all*, thought Green.

* * *

Hours later, Green and the second man were back. Dawn breaking in London signalled that the victim was not far from death. His only bit of luck was that he was in a coma, oblivious to anything, even the blood dripping from his eyes, nose, mouth and ears.

The victim had been a powerful man — he'd needed two people to hold him down when they grabbed him. Just an hour ago, he'd been flapping feebly against the restraints but even that had stopped.

The former DCI had an arrogant smirk playing on his lips and the light caught the cruelty in his face. He gestured at the victim.

"It's only very recently that this bleeding has happened. It's like he's taken extra-strength blood thinners." He waved his hand in the air, taking in the dingy back room of the building near Southwark Cathedral. "I have to say I wouldn't want my time to end this way, not in a shithole like this. I mean, can you imagine it? Bleeding from everywhere, even your bell end, probably? We can have a look if you like. No? I don't blame you. It would be nasty, very, very nasty. That would shake you up good and proper. And no one to hold your hand as you do an Elvis and leave the building." If anything, his smirk grew as he nodded in appreciation of his own humour.

As he spoke, a box on the floor near his feet thumped and juddered as the now captive snake hurled itself around in a blind rage. It was not a box anyone would want to open. The sheet-white man tried not to look at it.

Until very recently, Tony Green had been making a name for himself at Scotland Yard, hailed as a brilliant young thieftaker equally at home with the traditional law enforcement methods as with the digital tools provided by powerful databases. Green had been hailed as the modern face of the Met — the man the force needed after a series of scandals had laid the organisation low.

But all that had been exposed by the courage of Detective Constable Martha Munro, who had revealed that the real Green was a relic of the days when corruption was rife and attempts to clean up the force were rebuffed with brutal efficiency. Far from being the face of the future of law enforcement, Martha had shown Green was a murderous criminal mastermind who was up there with the worst of them. Overnight, he'd gone from shooting star at Scotland Yard to one of the force's most notorious criminals.

Standing alongside him, and shivering from both the cold and the knowledge that he was in the grip of a viciously deranged man, was Peter Smith — at least, that was the name he'd been born with, but no one in his circle called him that. They knew him as "the Banker", an accountant who specialised in hiding the vast profits generated by his criminal clients. Dirty money poured in — clean cash cascaded out.

Shaking violently, the Banker couldn't take his eyes off the dying man. He understood why he'd been brought here to witness this victim's final moments . . . It would be his turn next.

Unexpectedly, Green clapped him on the shoulder, making him jump. The Banker winced as Green's fingers dug in painfully.

"Look at me," said Green, his voice flat and menacing.

The Banker made eye contact. What he saw in that pitiless gaze drained the tiny hope he'd been clinging to. He was sweating profusely, dark stains showing around his armpits. He might have fallen if Green hadn't been clutching him so tightly.

The former detective's expression changed to exaggerated thoughtfulness. "You know, I can't decide which is worse. The actual bite itself, the waiting to get bitten or knowing you are going to die." He narrowed his eyes. "I suppose that fairly soon you'll get to experience all three of those things. You can let me know."

The Banker began to whimper. He was completely terrified and quite beyond caring how obvious his distress was.

Green took a backward step. He'd already had one pair of shoes spoiled by urine. "Tell you what," he said. "This is a big decision for you . . . I'll give you a couple of hours to think it over."

The Banker had gone grey and cold sweat suddenly drenched his forehead, dripping on his light blue shirt. He muttered something incomprehensible.

"What did you say? I can't understand you."

More mumbling.

Green leaned closer. "Say again. Don't be shy."

The Banker licked his lips but no sound came out.

"Perhaps water would help." Green passed him the bottle he was holding.

The Banker drank slowly, the liquid finally allowing him to find his voice. "I'll tell you everything . . . just keep the snake away from me," he managed a hoarse whisper.

It was enough. As Green absorbed the information his eyes narrowed in satisfaction.

CHAPTER 1

Die, Bitch.

It was the same message every time. The sender used a red marker pen to make it look like blood was dripping off the hand-printed words on the thick white paper. It was crude but effective, aimed firmly at Martha Munro and sent by a man consumed by the desire to kill her.

Martha sighed as she picked up the latest batch of messages lying in the hallway and tossed them in the bin. She knew who they were from — disgraced ex-cop Tony Green, now on the run after she had exposed the corrupt web he had spun at the heart of Scotland Yard. He'd got away with it for years, generating millions and millions. If he ran into trouble then a brown envelope stuffed with cash always worked . . . until Martha turned up. "Martha fucking Munro. So good ice wouldn't melt." She was so honest, her friends could trust her with anything, so loyal that they would do anything she asked.

The latest arrivals had turned up this morning, delivered by a postman who had been cleared after background checks. She had received dozens over just a few months and she wished they would stop. Not because the words scared her. Not at all. She knew Green was suffering from significant mental health issues for which he needed help. What got on her nerves was the sheer relentlessness of it. Why did psycho killers have to be so obsessive?

The messages arrived every two weeks. Sometimes she got forty or more at a time. Never fewer than ten. Why couldn't they just have a fist fight to settle it? But he was too cowardly for that. Probably couldn't face the prospect of a good kicking from a woman. He did want her dead, though.

It was Martha who had caused him to run after her clever detective work exposed the way his criminal organisation had infiltrated Scotland Yard in order to manipulate the police. It was exactly as though the world-famous organisation had been infected with a virus that allowed Green and his small team free access to the force's resources. It was the greatest humiliation the Yard had ever suffered.

It had taken blood, sweat and tears to finally expose Green, forcing him to flee the building, barely a step ahead of the arresting team. Left behind were a handful of men and women tasked with staying out of sight, working for him undercover to try and move his accumulated wealth away from the UK.

Martha tossed the message into the waste bin. She knew she really should have shared all this with the police and her friends, especially Harry, but something held her back, a sense that this was how it was meant to be. It was her problem and she needed to fix it. She wasn't a superstitious woman, not exactly, but there was one saying that always gave her pause: "Nothing happens without a reason."

Martha had the sense that fate was going to play a big part in what happened next and she felt confident that she was meant to be the solution. She had no fears about this man. None at all.

Green would kill her or Martha would kill him.

Trusting the word of a man like Green was a fool's game, and she didn't waste any time on that. Although she showed unusual caution in checking the mail when it arrived.

She thought of Harry again. He would hate it that he had been kept in the dark. Martha tried not to think about it, really hard, but it was difficult. He had pretty much brought her up after her dad died and her mother was subsequently murdered. Their secrets were few. She couldn't help thinking about how he would react when it came out. He wouldn't get angry, though she could cope with that. It would be the disappointment at her breaking one of their golden rules: Never go alone.

She was genuinely torn. On one hand, if she stuck to the plan of not telling anyone, he would be kept safe. But if she told him about it, there would be no chance of keeping him on the sidelines.

And if worrying about Harry wasn't enough, extra doubt was creeping in. When Martha had first decided to keep the letters to herself it had seemed like a really positive and compelling thing to do. Now she wasn't so sure. She was keeping solid evidence to herself and, by doing so, adding an extra layer of complication. Harry had always drummed into her, "Keep it simple — jettison what you don't have or understand."

Anyone passing by at that moment would have seen a woman silently berating herself. It was getting too involved for one person. She needed to reset and tell him.

Fresh air, that would help. She would be grateful for the mental breather and it would allow her to enjoy looking at her surroundings.

It was that time of day when the spring sun shone through the trees to create pools of sunshine all along Idmiston Road. It was a moment that showed the terraces of Victorian houses at their best. It was where Martha Munro had been born, and raised, forming deep, happy memories. She should have felt safe in such a familiar place but, after all that had happened, she sometimes couldn't escape the feeling that someone was lurking in the darkness, ready to attack when she let her guard down.

Martha couldn't quite suppress a shudder as she remembered Tony Green left alone in this house with Betty. She didn't like to think about it, but she needed to constantly remind herself that he possessed formidable charm that worked just as well on a five-year-old as it did on fifty-year-olds. In short, she had become close to him, and would have been closer if her senses hadn't done their usual trick of holding her back. Which Martha was so glad for. Had she pursued the relationship she could have found herself talking to the police about corruption and murder . . . at the very least.

As Harry had put it, getting close to a murderous madman was never the best way to progress, even in the modern police force.

The one bit of good news was that her daughter had emerged as a better judge of character than she was. She recalled him visiting her home and drinking tea in the kitchen. He'd gone out of his way to make a fuss of Betty — she'd put up the barriers and held him at arm's length. A very good move as it emerged. Green was a key figure in the London crime network establishing a sort of concierge service for those who wanted to cash in their supplies of foreign money, or an unscrupulous billionaire looking to shift anything. He was a crime boss, a "Face", and was known to the small handful of Faces who controlled major crime around Europe, who all worked hard to keep their identities close, especially Green.

It was Martha, with a little help from a five-year-old, who had created the first crack in his defences. It hadn't been long before more appeared.

Despite striking such a powerful blow she had the strongest sense that now was not the time to rest on her laurels. She couldn't explain how, but she felt Green's influence rapidly expanding. It looked like he was on the move again.

This time Martha was ready. He might not be able to see the clock, but somewhere a very accurate timer had started counting down.

CHAPTER 2

A wry smile briefly lit Tony Green's face as he thought about the reputational damage he could cause.

Not that he'd bother with that. He wanted his money, artworks, jewellery and the top-secret files that he had hidden away.

His priority was to grab as many of his remaining assets as he could. There had been a recent incident where one of his vans had been stopped as it drove up the boarding ramp of the ferry at the port of Dover. The driver was still being held under some bullshit terror legislation.

Green might have allowed his temper to erupt but he held his emotions tight. When every tantrum costs you money it makes you think twice. And they no longer had the luxury of time. The capture of the van was the first arrest the Yard had made. More would follow.

Now his focus had switched to the paintings that they had just discovered. He didn't know much about art but he did like numbers. Very big numbers. According to the art specialist, one hundred million — or more. He liked these numbers a lot.

Just as he thought his day couldn't get any better, he remembered an issue that had been bothering him. The problem he faced was not about finding her. He knew where she lived, he'd even visited for Christ's sake. What nagged away was thinking about what he would encounter at Martha's home. A mix of Harry's team and specialist personal protection officers. The police were bad enough — armed to the teeth and happy to shoot if it came to it. But Harry's mob were frightening, especially since the old boy himself was taking a fully hands-on approach. They were always keen to get their hands on intruders, something the would-be raiders found extremely distressing.

What it boiled down to was no one wanted to force their way in, subdue Martha, Harry and Julie, fight their way back outside, hope to get through a fresh barrage from the outdoor team and try to find somewhere they could hide out. It was a suicide mission.

No matter how much he offered, no one was interested apart from a handful of losers who saw it as their last big chance to make a name for themselves. Privately, Green referred to these people as "the Fuckwits" but they were all he had.

He was thinking hard about what he could do when an idea hit him. Very quietly, he would let it be known that he had a Warhol original that was available as a bonus to anyone who succeeded in bringing her dead body to him. It was a considerable prize as he was already offering a million in cash.

He also wanted to increase the pressure. The moment he got back to London he'd sent Martha the first of several messages. They were short and to the point. *I'm going to kill you*, or, *The last face you see will be mine. Give yourself to me or I take your daughter.*

Sending threats was a part of the job he enjoyed and which generally caused panic among the recipients. Not Martha. As far as he could tell, his hate mail went straight into the waste bin.

The bloody woman seemed indestructible.

In the past, Green had tried more physical attempts to hold her back, culminating in the deployment of a kill team, which he had hand-picked.

He pursed his lips as he recalled what a fiasco that had been. Despite detailed warnings, the men, and it was often men in that line, had simply walked away from the mission briefing thinking there was no woman who could beat them. A brutal encounter with Julie had altered their perspective. The so-called professionals had found themselves being thrown around like feather pillows before being knocked unconscious by a range of street-fighting moves.

His people had failed miserably and a lot of that was down to that geriatric thug, Harry. Wherever his people went, Harry was always waiting. Sometimes on his own, sometimes accompanied by a mob of elderly maniacs.

Common sense told Green it was time to go. At this rate it was just a matter of time before he lost. But a couple of things held him back. He hated losing and was furious that he had so misjudged Martha.

CHAPTER 3

Tony Green watched through slitted eyes as one of his men put a bullet in the back of the Banker's head. It was a brutal reward for a man who'd just provided astounding information — better than Green had been hoping for — but the man had been naive to the point of madness if he'd thought he'd be allowed to just walk away.

The problem was the Banker himself, who was probably one of the best-connected people in London, at least when it came to people of the criminal variety. And these were the people that Green was keen to ensure never discovered he was back on the streets. He'd spent a lot of time leaving a false trail that would make his pursuers think he had fled abroad. He had indeed spent a few months flitting around Eastern Europe but now he had quietly come back to London. If he'd let the Banker go free, it was inevitable he would reveal that Tony Green had returned — something he wished to keep a lid on as long as possible.

He shrugged as he watched the Banker's body being dragged away. It wasn't fair, but life wasn't fair, no point in going on about it.

He turned his back on that and switched focus to the future. Running away had stripped him of authority. He could win it back. A couple of kneecappings would help that. But it would take time.

Since that bitch Martha had come into his life, just thinking about her sent his blood pressure spiralling, offering a real test of his recently acquired deep-breathing skills to stop him reaching an intense rage. He calmed quickly. The breathing helped.

Losing his temper only made him misjudge his enemy, and Martha was as formidable an opponent as he had encountered. If he was honest, she was the toughest he had ever faced and seemingly impervious to bribery, flattery or threats.

These thoughts acted like jumping into ice-cold water and he calmly turned to thinking about the Banker. He really had struck gold when the man started talking, spooked by the sight of the snake making its way towards him.

Green had been amazed at the extent of the information that had flooded from the Banker. He'd been hopeful that the man would be useful but this exceeded that. Much of the information would have to be left for another day. There simply wasn't time to deal with anything new. If it was true, and it would be, it would give him exactly what he needed. He would have storage space, places for his staff to eat and drink, every bit of technology he could want and secure communications. Best of all it was in central London.

He rubbed his hands together. Snapping back into the moment he looked around and picked out two of his men.

Green jerked his thumb over his shoulder. "You two, get over there and sort this out. I want both bodies dealt with in the normal way. No mistakes or it will be you with the snake next time."

Green headed outside and got into the back of a Range Rover, which drove him to his penthouse flat in the Battersea Power Station development. He'd left without sparing a second thought for the orders he'd just given, his mind slowly turning over the information extracted from the Banker.

As the car made its way through the traffic, he became aware that his cheek bones were throbbing. Ever since the series of operations to change his appearance, his cheek bones had become more sensitive. Sometimes, like now, they felt hot and tingly. It was all he could do to stop himself touching his face.

He guessed it was changes in temperature and atmosphere that triggered it. The run-down house where he'd ordered the Banker's killing had been cold and damp after years of neglect, while the luxurious car was warm and dry. He gave in to temptation and gently placed his fingertips on the affected part of his face. As always, the sensation of heat proved to be an illusion as his cheek bones felt quite normal, almost cool to the touch. Green thought this strange sensation was a small price to pay.

The Hungarian surgeon had assured him that not even his own mother would recognise him, and he was right. She'd walked right past him — had actually brushed against him. He hadn't reached out to stop her, only making sure that he looked totally different. She needed to remain ignorant so as not to give him away. It was only later he'd wondered what he'd have done if she had somehow, underneath all that prohibitively expensive reconstruction work, realised the man with a stranger's face was her son. He suffered a rare moment of self-recrimination as he knew he would have had to order her elimination. There could be no witnesses. None at all. It was why his thanks to the surgeon and his team had been to order their killing. Never leave a thread your enemies can tug away at. As far as he was concerned, you made your own luck in this life and if anyone got in the way, that was their lookout.

His thoughts turned once more to Martha Munro. For some reason he hadn't killed her when she first popped up and he'd lost count of the number of times he'd come to regret that odd moment of indecision. The daughter of the late Commander John Munro, the ruthless foe of bent coppers everywhere, Martha was proving to be an annoying chip off the old block.

Before his death, Commander Munro had run the Met's anti-corruption unit and had been hailed as a hero — by most people. Just not the ones he brought to justice. But he had his own way of operating and rarely followed the rule book. He wouldn't have survived the modern police, with its emphasis on detailed reports filed straight to the cloud. Instead, he kept his most sensitive information in two secret diaries, one Martha was aware of and one she wasn't.

For a while the second book had remained a secret until a tiny number of people picked up the faintest hint. Different people were interested for different reasons. The people who were featured in it by name, or had been led to believe they were, wanted to find out how damaging the information was. It was known that the Commander had done deals with some big fish in order bring down even bigger fish. In this line of work, it was very bad news to be outed as a rat — especially one who had been talking to the filth, and the Commander was said to have kept copious notes about the deals that had been struck. With a small but very wealthy group wanting to get hold of the book it soon became a valuable commodity. Even more so when the original hunters were joined by those who hadn't merited a mention at all but were exceedingly keen to find out who had been namechecked.

By sheer chance — and an extraordinary degree of blind luck — Green had managed to get his hands on the book while attempting to undermine Martha as she led a murder investigation. He'd been after the first diary when he'd discovered the existence of the second. This was a diary that listed corruption in the wider world of politics and finance. Even Harry, who had been an unofficial right-hand man to Martha's father — some said he was like a consigliere to Martha's father — hadn't known about it.

It was this diary that had led Green to the Banker, and from him he was now in possession of some extraordinary information that he hoped would finally allow him to see off Martha. He lay back against the soft leather of the seat and reflected on the strange way fate worked. It had taken a lot to create such an opportunity. For once, the smile that touched his lips was genuine.

He was looking forward to seeing how well Martha worked when she was constantly looking over her shoulder.

CHAPTER 4

Martha had just returned home from work when she heard the thud of the letterbox. She turned and looked. A single sheet of white paper was on the floor.

It read, *Good evening, Martha. I'm outside.*

Martha opened the door. A man who looked familiar to her was standing there. He looked older and heavier but even surgery had not been enough to remove the arrogant smirk.

The shock struck Martha like a hammer blow.

It was Green. She'd almost expected he would do this — turn up at her home to gloat. She had long sensed that he was incapable of a straightforward killing. Let's face it — he'd had enough chances to murder her. But he needed to put on a show, prove that he was the master criminal with a brilliant plan and the nerve to see it through.

He broke into her thoughts.

"Long time no see, Martha."

"It feels not long enough to be quite honest." She allowed a small smile to play on her lips, determined not to let him detect how hard her heart was pounding.

The tiniest flicker at the corner of his mouth showed she'd scored a hit. That was good, it demonstrated what a thin-skinned man he still was.

"I'll let you have that one, Martha, because it will certainly be the last free shot you get."

"I won't need free shots to get rid of bullies like you."

"Strong words, Martha," he said. "Strong words indeed." Green held her gaze for quite a while. "I came here to see how you are and let you know I've made all the arrangements." The smirk was now a leer.

"What possible arrangements have you made that I would be interested in?" As she finished, she picked her nose very slowly, examined what was on her finger and put it in her mouth.

He looked as though he might be sick. She picked ever more aggressively.

"Was there anything else? I need to wash my hair," said Martha.

"I just wanted to let you know that I am almost done here in London. Once I'm ready I will, as promised, kill you. Just me. I don't want anyone else to enjoy the pleasure of seeing you die."

Green gave a slight nod as if to confirm the arrangements in his head, turned from Martha and slowly walked down Idmiston Road.

CHAPTER 5

Martha was waiting in the kitchen for the others to come back, using the time to practise some mindfulness to allow her to process the encounter with Green and, more importantly, how she was going to break the news that she'd been keeping secrets.

The first person to arrive was Harry, early as usual. Martha couldn't be in a safer pair of hands. When she was a child, he was always there for her. He walked her to and from school, even making her meals if her mother was out. Martha adored him and their relationship had remained the same as she grew into adulthood.

But on the terrible day that Martha's mother was murdered, Harry had shown a different side — one that made it clear the men who had taken Betty and killed her grandmother would come to regret ever getting involved.

That was the day that Martha was to learn about the real Harry, known as "Harry the hat" by all South East London gangsters.

She discovered he had been one of the most feared gang enforcers south of the river, a life he had turned his back on to keep a promise made to his dying friend, Commander John Munro: *"Keep my daughter, Martha, safe . . . at all costs."*

From that moment on their lives were to take them in directions that would put them on a collision course with some of the most ruthless criminals to be found anywhere. Most people would have grabbed the chance to run. Not Martha and Harry. They would stay and fight.

At least she had finally understood why so many people crossed the road when they saw Harry. The teddy bear of a man she thought she knew could turn into the most fearsome predator who gave no quarter.

There were two more things she would learn as the months went by. When she had first discovered she was being pursued by enemies of her father, she had found it almost impossible to process the idea. First, because of her father, she had enemies who wanted her dead. These were people she had never met, never seen and never knew about until one of their kind murdered her mother and snatched Betty, her five-year-old daughter.

There seemed to be a great many of these people who would emerge from the shadows and try to kill her. Some were even totally unknown to Harry. But they were powerful enemies, and what was driving them on, she would eventually learn, was a secret diary kept by her father that detailed all the payments he had made to police officers, politicians and even members of the judiciary.

Before his death John Munro was the man who policed the police. He'd been lauded for his work, but there was another side to him. Put simply, he was a maverick who did things his own way. Sometimes that meant looking after one criminal to catch another.

It was the information about who had been paid and how much that would eventually put his family in danger. When details emerged about his diary there was panic — no one wanted to be exposed as a rat who helped the police. Some of those named went after Martha simply because she was alive and might know something.

After many fearsome struggles, Martha had finally discovered who was the "Alpha Rat", a former copper called

Tony Green, who had thrown everything he had at seeing her dead. It was a frightening time and without help from Harry.

The end game was approaching fast and she needed to be ready. She had just four people in her team, including herself. Harry was now joined by the extraordinary Julie, who Martha owed her life to after a death attempt in prison, and Martha's ex-husband Justin was on her side too.

She would be relying heavily on Harry to provide extra muscle and protection. She wanted Harry and Julie as the last line of defence, in the hope that anyone getting that far would have already taken such a battering, they would be easy to deal with. Even more amazing were the number of people who owed Harry a favour. It meant not only was he providing well-disciplined and heavily armed "troops", it wasn't costing her a penny. Harry was sorting out the details — she had asked him to take charge of the extra men and women.

Despite the constant pressure, Martha found time to spare a few minutes thinking about her future. She needed to start putting herself first and she knew the future was a family life with Justin and Betty.

But there was just one way this was going, and it would end in a bloody battle between herself and Tony Green. No one else. Green wanted her dead — he was obsessed with killing her. Martha was more than aware of this, as Green had been sending her messages for some time. She had kept them to herself because her friends would be furious and try to attack him. And this highlighted the contradiction that she was experiencing. On the one hand, she was desperate for help from all her friends. On the other, she didn't want them to take any risks at all.

Martha against Green was personal. She knew that this fight was to the death. Neither of them was safe until the other was dead, and God help anyone who got caught in the middle.

CHAPTER 6

Not a word was spoken as the card was passed around and studied closely for clues. First up was Harry, then Justin and finally Julie. The big woman had made it just as Martha started to explain what they were doing. No one fidgeted or gazed out of the window. They were here to work.

Martha picked up the card, took a deep breath — it was time to tell the team the truth. "This is from Green himself."

It was Harry who was the quickest to work out what she was talking about. "Have you two been in contact in some way?"

Martha let the tension build a little and noted that Julie seemed especially keen to see what came next.

"Yes, it's true. I have been in very limited contact with Green. I was hoping that if I kept everything low key, it might entice him to be overconfident. And I was happy to go along with that."

You could have heard a pin drop in the silence that followed. Eventually it was the calm voice of Justin who asked, "When did all of this start? I mean, not telling us about being pals with a serial killer!"

Martha blushed in the face of this rebuke and held up her hands. "Guilty as charged, I'm afraid, but it's time to put that straight now."

As she looked at Harry, Martha could tell from his eyes that he wasn't pleased.

"I know it looks bad, but I wanted to keep you guys out of danger as much as possible. But looking at all of you now I can see that should be the other way around."

The comment brought a hint of a smile to Harry and she seized her moment to push the conversation along. "There is one more thing I need to tell you. Green turned up here this morning."

As she waited for the group to calm down, her mind drifted back to three years ago and the moment that marked the turning point from her old life to her new one.

Following her sentence at the Old Bailey, she was still numb with shock as she was driven through the main door of the high-security prison HMP Bronzefield. But her problems were only just beginning. Her enemies had let it be known within the prison community that there was a price on her head — payable on death.

The speed of events had knocked her sideways. One minute she was in an Old Bailey courtroom, the next she was fighting for her life . . . and not doing anywhere near as well as she needed to. Her combat skills would help for a while but they'd never keep her safe in the long term.

It was Harry who had saved the day. He knew a bloke who could reach inside the prison and get messages through. Harry was looking for help, would pay well and, best of all, whoever saved Martha would have Harry's undying gratitude.

The woman who stepped forward was called Julie and she was the biggest, toughest woman Martha had ever met. So tough that most of those who fancied a pop at the bounty suddenly lost interest. Those still keen tended to be the most desperate, backed up by a few chancers. They all came to regret their decision. Julie's motto was "Go in fast, go in hard, stop when they stop."

It was a quite remarkable performance and left Martha short of the words she needed to describe what had happened. "It was incredible" was the best she could come up with.

Martha, not unnaturally, wanted to shower gifts over this guardian angel but Julie was a woman true to herself. She'd stepped in because she wanted to. Never mind who she'd saved. But, in doing so, she had begun a powerful friendship between the two women, who would come to realise that in each other, they had met their kindred spirit.

Meanwhile, Harry had boosted their tiny team when he'd persuaded Martha to bring her ex-husband, Justin Baghwat, back into the fold. He had computer skills that no one else could match, and more importantly Harry liked him almost as much as Betty, who loved her father with a deep passion that was returned in equal part.

Justin had fallen out with Martha in an argument about him smoking cannabis. Justin was in the wrong but couldn't bring himself to apologise. The fight had escalated with his sad, but almost inevitable, departure.

Now he lived nearby and had had time to reflect on what had happened, he regretted the loss of his family.

CHAPTER 7

After her release from prison Martha's story became known to the wider world and Martha had, for a short while, been a major attraction on social media. To her enormous relief, she was quickly usurped by a seventeen-year-old darts player. As the attention switched to him Martha was able to hold meetings with the top players at Scotland Yard, including the Commissioner. She was also seen by a man and woman who said very little before leaving. Meanwhile, she was told the force was fully behind her, looking for the best way to utilise her talents and, on one occasion, the Commissioner had personally assured her she would be kept safe.

She would have welcomed this in another life, but after her recent experiences, she viewed these declarations of support with, at best, a degree of scepticism and, at worst, part of a wider plan designed to destroy her. She felt unable to trust people and most of them she had known for a long time. Her faith in her senior colleagues was put under enormous pressure after the latest escapade involving Green.

The HR team seemed especially discombobulated and clearly struggled to establish what to do with Martha, until finally they suggested that she spend time on gardening leave at home. Officially, it was said to allow protection teams to keep a close watch but she rarely saw them. She wasn't too bothered — she had her own protection. And being at home on her own gave her a chance to think. Even if this was the third time she'd been placed on leave.

For Martha, it was a case of keeping her eyes on the prize. It was a throwaway remark from Harry that had put her back on track. Over dinner at her home, Harry had been talking about people setting goals that were so high they were impossible to meet. If you set the goal too high, then the added pressure tended to defeat you.

It was like a light coming on. Green had made her lose the plot. She wouldn't quite go as far as ignoring her instincts but she now tried to take a much broader approach to judging people. Take Green — she had ignored the way he asked constant questions and she now saw that as a mistake.

Green was dangerous and cunning but she did have a major advantage. She too was also dangerous and cunning, and men like Green couldn't imagine being outplayed by a woman. If Martha was careful, that might make the difference between life and death for her.

She was mulling this over when she remembered she now had her own secret weapon in Justin. He was another one who was often ignored because of his gentle nature and stature — he was a couple of inches shorter than Martha. Having him back on board was invaluable. He was much braver than anyone suspected and knew how to keep a cool head.

CHAPTER 8

Twenty-five degrees Celsius, London was off to a hot and glorious spring. Martha was hot but far from glorious. She hadn't slept for days. The doctor had offered sleeping pills, which she'd rejected. She wasn't against controlled drugs but she'd asked the medic if instead of pills he had anything involving non-medicated treatments. He'd handed her a leaflet. She'd thanked him and left. She'd do her own research. An hour or so on the net and she had decided a long walk before bed was the trick. She'd told Harry she'd start tonight by going out around 10 p.m., which had nearly caused him to have heart failure. He'd insisted he come along. Martha didn't mind. Harry was perfect company for a nightly excursion. He knew when to keep quiet and tonight she was driven by a powerful need to get outside.

Martha set a good pace. She had headed off to Dulwich Village, then walked towards Camberwell for a while before turning back to head for home. If anything, her pace got faster on the return. She showed no concern for Harry and she didn't need to — he might be giving away fifty-plus years but all that did was give her a chance.

Coming close to the village, a gang of five men in their late twenties appeared. They were out for trouble and, unfortunately for them, they had found it in Martha, who was ready for a fight.

"Will you look at this?" said the leader.

"He's out with his little niece." He looked behind him. "What do we think, boys — should he be taking this girl home?"

Harry said nothing, just indicated with his hand for Martha to take the lead. She walked slowly towards the youths.

"She's saving us the trouble of having to go and get her. We should—" His words stopped as Martha punched him hard in the testicles. Anticipating his collapse, she expertly jabbed him in the nose, the sound of crunching bone apparent over the whimpering.

That was the leader down, but Martha wasn't slowing. She dummied to throw a punch at the next pair, who were standing far too close to make the most of the numerical advantage. She grabbed the back of their heads and smashed their faces together. Then she did it again.

Blood, teeth and even bone were on display. So were the heels of the last pair. But slow, oh so slow. Martha caught them in no time. The duo were panting hard enough she could almost imagine their hearts thumping inside their chests as they worked overtime.

Punch or kick? She went for the kick in the testicles before slamming their faces together. Okay, it wasn't really that different, but why change a winning formula.

As they dropped to the ground, she turned and walked back to Harry.

When he was in earshot she said, "That's the type of therapy I needed."

Harry snorted loudly and headed for home. Martha, meanwhile, was thinking that she really owed Harry an enormous debt that could never be repaid. Not the least of which was having taught her a formidable array of fighting skills. And he was a fabulous teacher, insisting she keep going until she had everything right. As a child, he had nearly driven her mad as she learned the individual skills she needed. But they were both determined and it was soon obvious she was one of the most accomplished fighters he had ever worked with. Now she was at least his equal and he'd been at the top level for a long time.

Walking back, she couldn't help wondering — yet again — if she was making life too complicated. Even if she could persuade Harry to step back from the fight, and that was a big "if", she doubted that any general in history had ever won by taking their best fighters out of the battle.

She tried to think how her dad would have reacted to her plan. Incredulous would be putting it mildly. And he'd have been right except for one thing — he wasn't trying to ensure her friends didn't throw their lives away. He also didn't have to put up with the little internal voice that said, *If Harry and Julie don't do it, who will? You?*

"What did you make of that little lot?" said Martha. She was hoping she could swing the conversation round to the thought that these were the sort of thugs they would be up against.

"They were rubbish. I mean, you had to chase after the last two just so you could hit them. Hopeless."

She sighed quietly. This wasn't going to be easy.

CHAPTER 9

Julie and Harry were making themselves comfortable in Martha's kitchen. Bright-eyed and well-muscled, they were exactly the sort of people you wanted in a fight.

She needed to do a few chores, then she would join the others for a cup of tea. Justin was at his flat getting ready to leave.

Julie took a delicate sip of tea, which might have surprised those who knew her, then she put her mug down, cracked the fingers on both hands and gave Harry a quick glance.

Almost imperceptibly, he shrugged. A few seconds later he moved about one centimetre. Few people would have spotted that. Even fewer would have known what had just happened. Which was Julie kicking him in the shins. She'd done it very hard. He'd barely flinched.

"Come on, out with it," said Martha.

Harry narrowed his eyes at Julie, who managed to look quite innocent.

"What gave us away?" asked Harry.

"It was you, I'm sorry to say. Ever since my father died and you started looking after me, I have never seen you flinch about anything. You are not a flinchy kind of guy."

By now, Julie was crying with laughter. "Can I do it again?" she asked.

"Shall I get you an Uber?" Harry asked pleasantly.

"Ha, ha," said Julie. "You're suggesting I might need to go to hospital if I do this?"

"Not at all," said Harry. "If I do this, I shall carry you to the Uber, give the driver fifty quid and tell him to leave you at the furthest train, tube or bus the money will take you. You'll be asleep all the time so no worries there. And you would be fine, wouldn't you? You're always telling me no one ever dares mess with you."

A brief bout of eyeballing was interrupted by Martha.

"I thought one of you was going to tell me something."

There was something about her tone that made them pay instant attention, and it was a tone neither of them had heard before. Harry looked briefly at the woman he cared for as much as if she was his own daughter. The glance was enough to show him something had fundamentally changed. She looked older, angrier and more determined.

Martha raised an eyebrow. She'd asked a question.

"Probably best if Julie tells you," said Harry. "But you should know, this came from Julie and I."

Julie, a giant of a woman who prided herself on her collection of tattoos and body piercings, craned her head in the direction of the oven. "The pizza will be ready—" she glanced at her phone — "in ninety-two seconds. Do you mind if I have a slice or two before we chat? I'm starving."

She watched Julie carefully handle the hot food and pass it around. It was a familiar domestic scene, and as she took the proffered slice, she smiled. She must make the most of evenings like this. It was unbearable to contemplate but they might not make it through the next few days.

A cold shiver ran over her like someone walking over her grave.

CHAPTER 10

Martha really needed to talk to Justin.

It had just gone noon when he arrived at Idmiston Road to be warmly greeted by the others. Martha's heart did a small flip at the sight of her former husband. She realised that she was falling back in love, and what a time for it to be happening!

Meanwhile, Julie had been persuaded to hand over the beer she had grabbed from the fridge. Until this was over they were staying sober. Reluctantly, she put the bottle back. She was saved from further temptation when Harry insisted it was time for the pair to leave for a couple of meetings.

As much as Martha adored them, she was pleased to watch Julie pulling the front door closed behind her. She turned her attention to preparing fresh tea, reflecting that she and Justin now spent more time talking than ever before. Martha smiled at the irony that she and Justin had some "home alone time" just as they had the least opportunity to use it.

She took a deep breath. "What do you do about a problem called Harry and Julie?"

Justin didn't speak for just a moment. "This is incredibly difficult, I don't understand why you would find them a problem."

"Okay, let me put it another way and you may have to put up with a bit of repetition. Tony Green is a seriously bad man and has made it his nasty little life's mission to kill me, and he would like to do that as painfully as possible but if there's no time, he will settle for a bullet in the back of my head.

"There can be no talking him out of this. It's going to come down to one conclusion — either I die or he does.

"This is something that I have been thinking about since Tony Green went on the run, and I have only one wish — to keep you all safe."

"My God," said Justin. "I can see why it's been such a dilemma for you. I know from my own personal experience that Harry doesn't take kindly to being told what to do about anything and it would be the same for Julie. But if it came to your safety. Well." He shrugged and sat down with a sigh.

Martha looked at him. "Not being rude but I didn't think you would be able to come up with a solution for something as complicated as this — at least not straight away.

"And as we have already said, Harry won't just give in and leave you to it." Martha noted how pale Justin had become. It was a lot to absorb but she hadn't finished yet.

"There's a bit more," she told Justin. "Julie is made from the same stuff. The only running she'll do is towards trouble. So that's two of them who won't do as they're told."

It took a moment for Justin to reply. "I find it almost impossible to call those two a problem," he finally said.

Martha sighed heavily. "That's what I have turned over and over in my mind. They may be causing a problem but to say it is their fault, that's rubbish."

She waited for him to look up. Then she knelt in front of Justin and rubbed her hands on his knees. "Let me give you something else to throw in the mix. After this, I want us to get back as a family. There is no other man that either Betty or I would want in our lives. But if anything happens to me then I want you to move into this house and care for our daughter."

33

Justin's expression flip-flopped through amazement and apprehension. If this hadn't been so serious, she might have laughed but she could see him gathering his thoughts and kept quiet.

"I can think of nowhere that would be better off without you in it. Nowhere at all. And we all know the same goes for Betty," said Justin. "As much as I love you, I don't think it's half as much as our daughter feels.

"But there is one thing you can be sure of. I will always have time and space for that little girl. And if you can't be there, I will do my best to take your place."

The silence that followed was profound. Martha realised that she needed to speak, or she would cry.

"Look, this is complicated and I need a second. I may not get all the right words so please be patient with me."

"Take all the time you want," said Justin. "But know this . . . the answer will still be yes."

CHAPTER 11

Justin drew a breath and let it out. Martha was filling the kettle.

"I don't know about you, but I could really do with more tea."

"Yes please," said Justin, suddenly realising how dry his mouth was.

Martha handed over a steaming mug. Justin blew gently on his hot drink and then put it down next to him. He looked at Martha in a careful way, as if he was judging her mood before asking his next question.

"Can I ask you something that may make you cross?"

"No worries," said Martha.

He reached for his tea then stopped. Nothing to be gained by waiting.

"The first thing is that I thought you laid out the issue really well and it needed to be said. Whatever happens, Betty and you need to walk out of here and so do the three of us, and right now it feels like we don't have a way of doing that or finding anyone we can talk to about it."

Martha was looking at him unwaveringly. He needed to stop prevaricating.

"How do we stand with the police? Some people might say that protecting the five of us is exactly what they are here for."

There was a silence. He didn't dare look at Martha.

Finally she answered. "I don't wish to be rude, but you have met everyone, haven't you? I mean, do Harry, Julie or me, come to that, look like they need police protection?"

"That's not what I meant," he said, glaring at her.

She winked at him. "I was just checking my stroppy ex-husband was still here."

He rolled his eyes. "Just answer the question."

"Okay. Fair enough," said Martha. "I'm not yanking your chain when I say that the police cannot be trusted, at least not until they've been checked out. To be honest, I'd sooner leave Betty with a pack of real-life wolves than most of those scumbags."

"Well at least we're clear about that," said Justin. "I had a feeling you might say no and you did. A very big NO. That leaves me one other thought."

"Go on," said Martha, her eyes bright.

"We may have to go on the run."

Martha stood up, walked over to Justin and kissed him lightly on the forehead.

"Look, we don't need to worry about that immediately," she said. "But I do want us to get our ideas out there while we have time to think about it. Now you have started the thought process I now need to find out what Harry and Julie have been up to and which direction they think we should go."

CHAPTER 12

"You did what?" asked Martha.

"We went and rattled his cage."

Martha closed her eyes for a moment. It was peaceful. She hated every aspect of this but especially the constant anxiety over whether they were doing the right thing. Despite what she'd told Justin, how many times had she woken in the night worrying that Betty might be safer under the protection of the police?

She shivered lightly. They'd had this conversation so many times and the answer was always the same. Yes, in theory, the police should be involved. But there was a problem, a very big problem in going down that path — Tony Green and his network of corruption. He pierced the Yard at so many levels that no one could be sure where his people were. As Harry had once put it, you could surround Betty with the best firearms unit the Met could provide, but it only needed one member of the team to be corrupt and she would be in even worse danger.

Now Harry was telling her that he and Julie had been engaging with Green's people. She didn't know whether to laugh or cry.

She took a deep breath and when she reopened her eyes the sparkle was back. She could never quite stop a bout of introspection, but she didn't let it take over.

She looked at Harry and Julie. "Well, I guess congratulations are in order. I've not heard of people making it into his gang and coming back out. At least, still breathing that is." She braced herself. "Okay. Give me the gory details. Don't spare me anything. And did you pick up any clues as to what Green's up to?"

"We did get something," said Harry. "But calling it a clue might be stretching the definition of the word. We'll give you the full, unedited version. See what you think. But as I said, we really don't know much at all. It's gone very quiet or, as you might say, Martha, it's so quiet something has to be going on."

CHAPTER 13

Martha and Justin listened intently as Julie and Harry deconstructed the way they had identified a potential weakness in the gang's security.

"So go on, then, Harry," Martha said. "How did you work it out?"

"It was thanks to Julie, actually," he said.

Julie gave him a quizzical look.

"You remember that over-muscled creep you had to slap around when we initially started going after Green?" he asked her.

"I certainly do," said Julie. "He started snivelling in next to no time. I can't believe he was being paid to act as a bodyguard."

"Yup, that's the one." Harry grinned again. "Well, in between the snot and the pleading he said that Green is a total control freak. Luckily, Julie had left the sniveller in one piece, more or less, and he talked us through who was who. The great thing about talking to junior people is they are less likely to kill you on the spot since they always need to refer upwards — at least they do if they want to carry on living. Once we'd identified a way of using their system to reach the top, the really important thing was making sure the message got through as we intended.

"You have to keep it simple and easy to understand, and most of all, it must be obvious that Green himself needs to see it."

"What did you say?" asked Martha.

"Simple. We got a 'Love London' postcard and put *'Hi Tony. Good holiday?'* on it. That should get Green's attention, make him focus," said Harry. "He'll be thinking about how we got the message through. My guess is we're the first people who have ever managed to penetrate his organisation. The first thing he'll do is order a security review and I wouldn't want to be the man in charge of that. Green doesn't like failure and will be itching to make an example of someone."

Martha was looking like a great weight had fallen off her shoulders. "You seem to be turning into the ideas man, Harry. Although I'm very conscious Betty's arriving home shortly, so we need to crack on."

"Actually, Harry, it was you and your people who did most of the work," said Julie.

Martha nodded in agreement. "Yes, Harry, it was your plan and you're quite right — it worked." She waved her now half-empty mug at him. Harry was famous for his builder's tea, which Julie claimed was strong enough to wake the dead and was certainly the perfect antidote to a bout of navel gazing.

"Up to a point," said Harry. "But I think the lesson we learned is that getting alongside Green is close to impossible. So, given that Betty's safety is paramount, how do we keep her safe? Do we keep her here or send her away?" He paused and stared intently at Martha. "This is your call, but I don't think she would understand being brought home and then sent away almost immediately. I mean, I wouldn't like it myself."

Betty had spent the last few months with some friends of Harry, and Martha couldn't wait to have her daughter back with her. But was her desire to have her back under the same roof selfish? Did it put Betty at risk?

There was probably only one answer. Yes. She would be putting her in harm's way, though oddly Martha could almost trust Green over this — Betty was not on his list, so no problem. Even the time she had been snatched had been down to rogue operators and Green didn't allow that type near his organisation.

Another factor about Betty that people failed to consider was that she really wanted to come home. Every time she got the chance she would call Martha and plead to come back. Then she'd call Harry, then Julie, then Justin. She was relentless in the way that only small children can be.

She laughed to herself. Betty had been stashed away in some idyllic spot in the countryside near Birmingham. It was a paradise with a herd of reasonably friendly alpacas who now loved Betty as the official feeder. If it was her, she'd have stayed. Not Betty. She wanted out — although she did ask if should bring her favourite animal home. Freddie the funny alpaca.

Martha took a sip of her tea. Trust Harry to get to the heart of things. And trust Harry to present the issue of looking after Betty as having one answer and one alone. She watched him blowing on his own tea to cool it down and thought, not for the first time, he wasn't a man who ever made it easy — and she wouldn't have him any other way. She was deep in thought and unaware of how long she had been quiet.

"How long would it take to make this place our stronghold again?"

It was a key question and Harry had the answer. "Literally no time at all."

"Talking about hand-picking security reminds me of a course run by MI5 that I was sent on," said Martha. "One of the instructors made a point that the most important thing when it came to protection wasn't the gear you used, it was the people. Have the right people with the right commitment and that's the best you can hope for. Actually, there was a bit more to it, but you get my drift. With you two I couldn't put myself in safer hands."

"So, you're happy for Betty to stay here?" said Harry. "You're sure you don't want to think about it a bit longer?"

Martha looked over to Justin, who gave her the slightest nod. "How long have I got to make this decision?"

"At least five minutes," said Harry with a grin.

"Don't need it. I've decided, you can make that a yes," said Martha.

She knew it was fanciful, but as she spoke, Martha thought the atmosphere lightened and the house got brighter. Harry and Julie looked delighted at the call.

A thought struck her. "What about Justin? Does any of this place him at more risk?"

"Not at all. I'll keep him safe," said Harry, who had grown fond of her ex-husband in recent times. Justin was in fact a valuable team member with his knowledge of IT and he also had a calm manner, which others picked up on.

"But do we have any sense of how Green views him?" persisted Martha.

"Julie and I thought about that and it's a bit of a grey area," said Harry. "We're all in the firing line for different reasons but hopefully we can keep Justin further away because he will be looking after Betty and also not on the front line like the rest of us." Harry thought about what he'd just said and gave a rueful smile. "You know what I mean."

Martha pulled a doubtful face, not totally convinced by the logic but Julie held a hand up. "You can't factor in every variable but we do know that Green is utterly single-minded. He wants you and you alone. That's where his focus is."

"You know how to make a girl feel wanted — just not in a good way," said Martha. She stood, then, at a loss for what to do, filled the kettle and checked the biscuit barrel for Betty's favourite chocolate fingers. It was full. "Does anyone fancy a quick cup of tea before Betty arrives?"

"I bought those yesterday," said Harry, nodding to the biscuit barrel.

Martha didn't reply. She was too busy adding chocolate fingers to the list of things she wished she hadn't eaten that day.

At that moment, the front doorbell rang. Martha's heart jumped. Betty was here.

CHAPTER 14

London is a big city, an easy place to lose yourself in. Or at least it used to be before it became home to cameras of every type. From the basic setup covering the front door of your home, to sophisticated surveillance systems incorporating AI-powered software, Big Brother could track your movements wherever you went.

It has been claimed that London is home to more cameras than most other world cities. While Tony Green doubted anyone had actually counted, he knew from his days in the police just how comprehensively covered London was. He also believed that the security services were not above tapping into private networks to give them eyes everywhere all the time. It wasn't just cybercriminals who tapped into the growing trend for people to have digital cameras fixed to front door cameras. They were remarkably easy to hack, allowing all sorts of people to piggyback off domestic Wi-Fi systems.

Tony Green was well aware that unfriendly eyes could be looking at him through a whole range of lenses. And when you needed to remain out of sight, that was a problem. For months now he and his team had been on a war footing, only moving around when it was necessary, travelling by vehicles with blacked-out windows and even taking such rudimentary precautions as wearing dark glasses and hats pulled down to conceal the top half of the face. The reality was such things made small differences, especially now that AI systems were being rolled out to work alongside facial recognition systems. Small things were better than nothing, and doing nothing was never an option since it always made your enemies think they had a chance of bettering you — and it made your worker drones lazy, something he couldn't abide.

From time to time, he liked to punish members of his team just to keep the others on their toes. They didn't even need to make a mistake, just find themselves in the wrong place at the wrong time. Plus, it was inevitable someone would make a mistake, which gave him the opportunity to order a punishment beating. Sometimes, he would carry them out himself. Show him a better stress buster than a well-judged nose breaker. It tended to create an air of paranoia, but he didn't care. Some people argued that paranoia was a bad thing. Not Green. It was thinking about all those people who wanted to put his head on a spike that kept him vigilant and safe.

Most of the time, he enjoyed staying a step ahead of his enemies. The challenge made him feel alive, especially given that he was effectively playing for his life. One misstep and that would be it. But soon he would be leaving all of this behind. He would be heading to a remote part of the world free from prying eyes.

He shrugged the daydream aside. He needed to be here as he set about dismantling his empire and that was going to take a few months more. Just moving several tons of precious metals, including gold and platinum, and jewels including diamonds and emeralds, required detailed planning and took up time and resources . . . Then there were the works of art, the car collection — he even had a huge quantity of fine wine safely stored away. As for property, he'd decided early on to keep his property empire.

There was still much to be done and there could be no question of anything being left behind. He'd worked too hard to let it go. But his team would need to perform at the top of their game to pull this one off. Shifting such a huge amount would attract attention at the best of times, now it would be much harder. For instance, one of his favourite routes in and out of England was the container port at Tilbury, on the Thames estuary. The problem he faced was there being too many people who suspected he favoured that route. All anyone checking would need was a big wad of cash mixed together with a few threats and they would know all about his operations at the Essex port. He was going to have to be creative and, thanks to the information supplied by the Banker, he might just have obtained what he was looking for. Best of all, if it worked out, he would have the time to do some serious thinking about Martha fucking Munro.

So far he'd had to concentrate on his assets, but at the back of his mind was the thought of how he was going to exact his revenge. Slow and painful sounded good but he wasn't picky . . . just painful would do. He shook his head. Painful, yes, very painful. But dragging it out as long as possible, that was what he really wanted.

Green mentally slapped himself for letting thoughts of revenge cloud his mind. Martha would get what was coming to her, he was going to make absolutely certain of that, but taking care of business was more important than pleasure. Having said that, he did need to make time to think very hard about the information from the Banker because that might prove the answer to his dreams. If it was true, it would speed up his departure and give him more time to sort out Martha.

Today was a site visit but he was confident enough that it was going to prove perfect that he had already ordered his latest round of "cleaning house" by getting rid of the few remaining people who knew about it. Very soon he would be the only person in London who knew the secret and — more importantly — how to access it. It was the ideal hiding place, in plain sight.

"We're here, sir." He was so lost in thought that his driver's voice made him start. He had almost forgotten he was in a car. He looked out of the window. As instructed, the chauffeur had pulled up at the steps leading to the Science Museum. From here Green was on foot. It was a decent walk, not too far but enough to stretch his legs and give him some thinking time.

Most importantly, he no longer went anywhere on foot without checking if he was being tailed. The longer the walk, the harder it became for any surveillance to stay hidden. Quickly looking around, he set off.

CHAPTER 15

Martha was taken aback when she opened the door to find a man about six feet tall standing where she had expected to see Betty. He was as ordinary-looking as anyone she'd ever met, with a pale round face, sandy hair and light blue eyes. He had no distinguishing marks that she could make out and just stood there without saying a word. He made no attempt to acknowledge her and simply pulled a phone from his inside jacket pocket, which he ostentatiously studied as though it was the only thing that concerned him. But the oddest thing of all was that he managed to avoid making any overtly threatening gestures, despite standing right on her doorstep. It was clearly a performance designed to get under her skin and despite exercising rigid self-control, had she been holding a Taser, she would have shot him.

He made a non-committal humming noise, looked up and nodded briefly before saying, "You're Martha." It was a statement, not a question.

Martha took a step backwards. The more time elapsed, the more it became clear there was something creepy about this man and his robotic blandness. If things went downhill, she'd given herself room to manoeuvre. Nothing fancy — a well-placed kick in the balls was what she had in mind. This man hadn't said who he was but she knew exactly who'd sent him. Tony Green.

A thought struck her and she stepped forward again. Betty was due at any moment and if her daughter appeared, nobody, least of all this dickhead, was going to get in the way of their reunion.

She took a quick look around. Good. Just time to make this creep disappear.

The man spoke. "I'm going to take an envelope out of my inside pocket. Nothing to be worried about. It's not a weapon of any sort." Unlike the rest of him, his voice was deep and rich, like that of an actor who had had speech training. He withdrew a cream-coloured envelope.

Martha was on full alert. Trusting the word of a complete stranger, one sent by her enemy, Tony Green, would have been foolish. Instead, he held the envelope towards her, which, after a moment, she accepted. Job apparently done, he turned on his heel with a sort of snap that suggested he was ex-military and walked away. Reaching the pavement, he turned to the right towards Tulse Hill and was quickly out of sight.

Martha stood quite still and watched him walk away, the envelope held tightly in her right hand. She might have stayed there for a while longer but the spell evaporated as she heard Harry call her name. He was in the doorway to the kitchen and looked poised for action.

"There was a man here. Now he's gone," she said, making her way back to her friends. She handed Harry the envelope. "It's from our friend."

Harry studied it carefully as though it were a hand grenade and then opened it. He took out a sheet of paper, on which was printed the message: *I am going to make you beg for me to kill you. The first thing I will do is peel the skin off your face.*

"I'd like to see the little shit try and peel an apple before he starts on people," Harry growled.

"He's making a big mistake thinking I scare easily," interjected Martha, winning herself an approving pat on the back from Julie and Justin.

Harry looked as if he was going to say something but remained silent as he scrunched up the note. Martha looked at him quizzically, inducing a shrug.

"Go on," said Martha. "Out with it. I can tell something's on your mind."

"I was only thinking how much he likes playing games. I was thinking that perhaps it's time we joined in and played our own."

They all looked at Harry, who said, "That man at the door just then, we'll have caught him on the security system. If I can get him identified, then why don't I send someone to go and knock on his door? Just to let Green and his team know that two can play at that game."

"Phew," said Julie. "I like the way you're thinking . . . Can I be the one who pops round to say hi?"

"I wasn't thinking of scaring him to death, more of a gentle prod as it were," said Harry, who was keeping a determinedly straight face.

"You what?" said Julie. "You're seriously suggesting that I might frighten them? I don't think so and let's face it, it's better than you turning up. I can picture the scene — the door opens and you're there, smiling horribly. Then there's a loud crash as they faint dead away."

The banter between the pair was cut off as the front doorbell rang, stopping any further conversation. This time, Martha opened the door to see her beautiful daughter standing there, accompanied by two security men tough enough to make even Harry think twice. Betty jumped into her mother's arms with a delighted squeal. Martha held her fiercely, like she really meant to never let her go. But her daughter was on a mission and wriggled free. Moments later, came sounds of joy from the kitchen as Betty saw Harry and Julie.

The noise increased when Justin walked in.

Harry caught Julie's eye, indicating they should leave. "We'll go and get some essential supplies, like chocolate cake. Back soon."

Making their way out, Martha noted that the two guards almost stood to attention as they caught sight of Harry. Not for the first time, she speculated that he must have been truly formidable back in the day when he was chief enforcer for the biggest criminal gang in South London. Even today, fifty years on, he exuded a menacing sense of coiled energy that could be unleashed at any moment.

"All right, lads," said Harry, addressing the two men who were acting like soldiers on parade. "Thanks for getting Betty back safely. Any issues at the school today?"

The biggest of the pair, who sported a double-broken nose said, "There was one thing, not the biggest deal, but since you ask, we had to chase off an expensive-looking Mercedes with blacked-out windows. We had never seen it around before and none of the other parents recognised it so we thought better safe than sorry. So we went over to talk to the driver, who drove off before we got a chance to see who they were."

Harry nodded. "Thanks, Eddie. If it happens again, let me know straight away."

Harry and Julie carried on walking down the road to stock up on supplies for Betty.

The little girl was in the process of checking out her room. "I want to make sure everything is as I left it," she stated solemnly.

"No worries there," said Martha. "I've been personally looking after it." She didn't mention her frequent visits to the empty bedroom so she could revel in the scent of her daughter. On the toughest days, the ones where she resented having ever heard of Tony Green, holding her daughter's pillow and taking in her smell had been the only thing that had kept her sane.

As she watched her daughter, a message popped up on her phone. It was from the Commissioner's office. Dame Paula Charteris, the head of the Metropolitan Police wanted to see her at Scotland Yard, tomorrow morning, 9 a.m. sharp.

Justin sensed it was something important. "Anything I should know?" he asked.

"I hope so, but it's a bit early to say. The Commissioner has asked to see me but no details yet," said Martha.

Further conversation was stopped in its tracks as Harry and Julie let themselves back in. "Anyone for freshly baked chocolate cake?" shouted Harry, prompting a one-girl rush from Betty. Martha almost pointed out that she was due to eat dinner in an hour but stopped herself with a wry smile. She would just enjoy the sight of her little girl tucking in.

Several hours later and Betty was finally asleep after insisting that every adult present read her a story. Fearing they would be there all night, Martha had negotiated a compromise — one story with each person reading a different section. As the story was nearing its end, Betty was fighting off sleep and only managed to stay awake long enough for a final hug and kiss from Mummy.

CHAPTER 16

Harry had completed his reading duties earlier and was downstairs making yet more tea when Martha walked back into the kitchen. It had taken all her willpower to leave her daughter alone. She doubted she could ever see enough of her little girl lying fast asleep in her own bed. She noticed Harry had turned slightly so he could both see her and keep one eye on the stream of freshly boiled water he was pouring into the teapot.

"If Paula Charteris wants to see you, that might be good news," he said. Harry had a habit of instantly picking up on conversations that had been interrupted. He stirred the teapot before adding, "I wonder if they have worked out that Green is back in town. Let's hope she's set up that special unit she promised weeks ago. You haven't even had some sort of update? Anything at all would be good. I wasn't expecting her to keep up a constant flow of information but we'd all really like to know what she's doing about finding Tony Green. Surely they must be doing something constructive, not just waiting with fingers crossed that he somehow falls into their laps."

"To be fair," said Martha, whose expression suggested it was the last thing she felt like doing, "she did warn me

I'd have to wait while the task force was set up. I guess you don't conjure these things out of thin air. And it's not as if I'm going to be running it, not even close. I'll just be one of the smaller cogs . . . She has no need to keep me up to speed with every last spit and cough."

She was talking about a plan to create a special task force of top operators from different fields, ranging from counter terror and gang busters to key players from GCHQ and Martha herself. At least, that had been the plan put forward a few weeks ago. The idea had two important strands. First, arrest Tony Green and bring him to justice. Second, try to detail how much damage he'd caused when he was still a police officer and establish if he'd left any Trojan horse operatives in place. The view was that while he might have fled far away — South America was a popular guess among investigators who fancied an all-expenses paid trip — it was highly plausible he had left some of his people behind. They would be keeping the lowest profile possible but at some point, they would have to stick their heads over the parapet.

Assuming that did happen, investigators were debating their options, which led to divided opinions. Some argued that the Trojan horses should be left in place so they could be carefully monitored. With careful handling, these people could be used to feed false information to Green and his operatives. The second viewpoint was blunter. Throw them in prison — a CIA style black site was a favoured place, especially if Green himself was among their number — and throw away the key. That was the view very much favoured by Martha, Harry, Julie and Justin.

Back in the real world, Martha watched as Harry finished making her tea and handed her a mug. Harry was not one to spare much thought to the new way of thinking that held people should drink less traditional tea and more herbal tea. She cupped both hands round the brew and took a small sip of the hot drink, blowing carefully to cool it down. She took another grateful sip, thinking today was not a day for calming chamomile.

She finished her drink and sat for a moment gathering her thoughts about Paula Charteris. Since she had mentioned Scotland Yard to Harry he was doing nothing to disguise his scepticism that they would ever do anything of real value. In recent days, he'd become increasingly vocal about the apparent lack of effort from Scotland Yard — and if truth be known, she too felt the Met was finding things to do rather than focusing on grabbing Green.

The issue was simple: the scale of Green's infiltration of Scotland Yard. Just who had he managed to corrupt during his time at the Met? At first, it had been tempting to assume that most of those he'd turned were relatively low-ranking police officers, sergeants and inspectors, with maybe a handful of superintendents or chief superintendents. Important people they might have been but they weren't quite the big shots who held the reins of power.

The more she thought about it, the more she realised how naive she had been. Green himself had been a chief inspector and could have gone much higher but chose not to, seeming to prefer the relative anonymity of his rank as a way of avoiding scrutiny. After all, who could have imagined that a chief inspector could wield the sort of influence that would interfere with policy making and even stop criminal investigations?

Once she accepted this line of questioning it was just a matter of following the money, or in this case looking at the command structure at Scotland Yard, starting at the top and working backwards. Looking at it this way, it wasn't such a long shot to wonder about the Commissioner herself and all the top-ranked officers around her.

She already knew that Green had access to huge sums of cash. If a large slice of that had been sent to Paula Charteris, then she would be the perfect person to carry out Green's wishes.

Of course, Martha had no proof this was the case but her instincts were telling her she needed to raise her sights. And while it might not be the Commissioner herself who was being paid off, what about her deputy? Or one of the many assistant commissioners and commanders? It was a frightening thought that could explain why Scotland Yard was dragging its feet. And she was not one of those who thought that just because Green had vanished, he no longer had any clout. She was quite certain that any interference, by whoever was responsible, was being done on his direct orders.

She'd been thinking about this for a while and it was time to share her thoughts with Harry, Julie and Justin. If she was right — and in her heart she knew she was — she had to accept that they faced formidable opposition that placed everyone in real danger. She had allowed the crazy idea that she could possibly negotiate with Tony Green to get in the way.

Not anymore. Actually, her daughter's return had got her thinking straight. She looked over at Julie and it was as though the huge woman was a mind-reader.

"Come on then, out with it. I can tell you've got one of those Martha brainwaves you need to tell us about."

"Am I that obvious?" replied Martha, who had now drawn Harry's attention. "I have been thinking and it's not making me happy. I think we are in the utmost danger."

Harry opened his mouth and she knew what he was going to say.

"You're about to ask how can it get worse? Well, it can. I can sense it. But that doesn't mean we give up. I have a plan. Let me run it by you."

Harry's eyes glittered. This was the Martha he knew.

CHAPTER 17

Tony Green had attended a countersurveillance course and the words of the instructors came back to him now: "Be natural." The key point they had made was to do nothing that might alert any possible tail. The chief instructor had put it quite amusingly.

"You've all seen TV shows where someone uses a shop window's reflection to check if someone is following them. Nice idea, it might even work. There's just one problem. You need to choose the right shopfront, and not just to get the angles right.

"If you are a bloke and they see you apparently looking at a women's clothing store, you're going to give the game away, make your tail back off, or, worse, decide that because they've been found out, they might as well get on the front foot and attack you there and then.

"So, take your time and make it look as natural as you can. Done right, you can lure your tail away and lose them in the crowds — or even deal with them more forcibly. But that's a different course.

"The big takeaway I'd like you to think about is this: If you can lose someone without making them certain you have spotted them, you create confusion and that always buys you time. Which might be invaluable."

Her comments had drawn an appreciative round of applause and as he recalled them now, Green was careful to prevent a smile breaking out. Wandering around London, on your own, with a big grin on your face was a surefire way to attract attention — you even ran the risk of having people cross the street to avoid you. Not good if the plan was to keep a low profile.

None of this deterred him from taking basic measures such as walking slowly and leisurely . . . a man with all the time in the world, stopping occasionally to admire a chosen shop window so long as it was displaying appropriate items like menswear. He also made a point of stopping to get his bearings, not trying too hard but sometimes looking to see if anyone was following him. He even thought about doing the occasional burst of power walking but decided that made him look exactly like he was trying to shake a tail. After half an hour of random ambling, he was reasonably confident no one was after him. Unless he was the subject of a major operation involving many spotters. But if he had that many people following then the game was up.

It never hurt to practise being careful. You couldn't always tell when it was needed and the prize at stake was worth making a bit of effort for.

Deliberately taking a roundabout route through this expensive part of London, he arrived at the house he had been looking for. A huge white stuccoed mansion, a typical style of the Borough of Kensington and Chelsea. He slowed his pace as he walked past. Another twenty paces and he stopped, dropping to one knee as he pretended to tie a shoe lace, giving him the opportunity to check his surroundings — all seemed quiet.

He made his mind up. It was now or never. His heart racing, he stood, turned and swiftly retraced his steps. Walking up to the front door of the property he opened it with a digital thumbprint he'd had taken from the Banker, swiping the image on a keypad to gain entry. There was tougher security to get through, this just got him into the hallway.

He closed the door and waited, adjusting his eyes to the gloomy interior. A brief shiver ran down his spine. This had once been the bustling home of a wealthy man. Now it was deserted and a thin layer of dust covered all the surfaces. He reminded himself to focus, not get distracted by the eerie silence. There was a sequence to follow and he needed to do it properly or he would be stuck here. He briefly wondered about the sense in keeping what he was doing from any of his team, then thought that if the worst happened, he'd have to call for help. He even considered pulling out and getting someone to enter ahead of him. What if there were traps to negotiate?

He shook himself. The Banker had been very precise about what he needed to do and Green had no fear the man had held nothing back. At the time, he was giving up the information he was in no state to lie. No, he would do this himself and do it alone. It was potentially the biggest prize to ever fall into his lap.

Taking a breath, he checked the front door was securely closed then pressed a button by the top hinge. It was a small button that no one would see if they didn't know exactly where to look. The Banker had explained that pressing the button set a clock running. Now, time was crucial. He needed to be precise and methodical.

He took out his mobile phone and started a countdown from thirty seconds. Eyes rapidly adjusting to the gloom, he looked round for Van Gogh's *Sunflowers*. It was exactly where he'd been told — in the centre of the wall on the right as you walked in. Carefully, since he didn't know if it was real or a copy, he took the picture off the wall, surprised at how heavy it seemed.

Moving the picture revealed the keypad he had been expecting. By now, ten seconds had elapsed and his countdown relentlessly moved to nineteen seconds. No need to panic, there was more than enough time left but he needed to crack on. It would be an absolute disaster if he lost out now. He quickly tapped in the code number from memory, careful to ensure there were no fat-finger fuckups.

He entered the seventh number and was about to tap in the last digit when he froze. Had he got it wrong? Cold sweat erupted and bathed his face.

He had four seconds left. A desperate thought surfaced. There was just time to back out and run away before he was sealed inside. His brain took over and, as the countdown hit three, he reached inside his jacket pocket, pulling out a sheet of paper. Two seconds. He unfolded the crisp sheet of paper — there it was, the last number. Eight for the final digit.

He entered the number just as the countdown hit zero.

He'd been warned there would now be a delay. For the longest five seconds of his life, nothing happened. Time slowed down until he was convinced he'd made a mistake and it was all about to go wrong. He was waiting for a green or red light flashing on the keypad.

"Don't be red," he said, unaware he was talking out loud. "Come on . . ."

The green light flashed. He let out a long breath and rolled his shoulders to relieve the tension.

He had one more task. The system now allowed him to tap in a new code, which is when he discovered, to his distaste, that his hands were damp with sweat. He rubbed them dry on his trousers, tapped in the new code then stepped back and took a more leisurely look at his surroundings.

So far, so good. He peered into the gloomy interior and stepped inside. Motion detectors picked him up and automatically fired up the lighting. One moment he could see very little, the next bright lights lit up a corridor laid with marble flooring. He could see a staircase, leading down, a short distance ahead. He wasn't given to superstition but as he walked down the corridor and paused at the top of the stairs, he was struck by an eerie feeling that he was the first person to see this in a few years.

Enough hesitation, he told himself, and made his way down. It was time to explore, to find out if this really was the answer to his prayers.

CHAPTER 18

Martha knew they were the perfect team to pitch ideas at since all three went straight for the big picture and tended not to get bogged down in details. It occurred to her that they looked like the three wise monkeys. With a slight smile, she decided Harry was "see no evil", Julie was "hear no evil", and Justin the "speak no evil" member of the trio. As if to prove her right, they all continued to watch her expectantly. But without a sound. All Martha could hear was the gentle hum of her fridge and the odd crackling from the child monitor they'd placed in Betty's bedroom.

Harry looked especially keen to hear what she had to say. Having known her literally all her life, he had learned to trust her intelligence and her instincts. She had the rare ability to pick out the points other people missed, allowing her to seemingly pluck ideas from thin air.

He noted the faintest of smiles drift across her face — and for the briefest of moments he could see the young girl she had once been, making him nostalgic for easier times. As for Martha, she could safely say that apart from time spent with Betty, being with these people, her closest friends, was when she felt her happiest.

"Let me set out my thinking," said Martha. "You three can tell me if it's any good or not."

No one spoke, everyone wanted to hear what she had to say.

"Before I get into the plan, I need to set out some worries. I'm increasingly confident that someone high up is under the control of Tony Green. Nothing else explains quite why the Yard is dragging its feet about setting up a special unit to hunt him down.

"I think there are a few reasons for that. If I'm right, and there are top people doing his bidding, then it's because they want to give him time to cover his tracks and hide everything he has looted over the years.

"While I'm certain he has been shutting down his operation, I'm just as sure that's not all he has been doing. After today's visit, he's starting to flex his muscles and feeling very sure of himself.

"We know he claims I'm his only target but I think that's untrue. In my opinion, he wants to annihilate us all."

She was glad to see the Harry and Julie were looking determined and showed no signs of concern. Justin was looking quizzical and was about to speak but she interrupted him.

"I was just about to get to you. It's the three of us who are the main targets, but if he does get to me, Harry or Julie, I'm worried that he may come after you and Betty. So our job is to make sure he doesn't get that chance." She took a sip of now cold tea to counter a tickling feeling in her throat.

"I'll try and explain that as best I can. Please bear with me since I obviously don't have any hard evidence, but I am confident my instinct is pushing me in the right direction.

"He wants me because I made the direct intervention that exposed him for what he is. A bent copper. Just that, nothing fancier. He's a bully with a lot of cash to throw around and a keen eye for spotting those people who are open to bribery.

"He wants Harry and Julie because they were directly involved in what happened and he wants them to pay the price for taking him on. Like I said, he's a bully and one who's never received a taste of his own medicine before. Now he has and he doesn't like it." She took a long pause before she spoke again. "I'll admit that this is all based on instinct . . . I haven't asked him yet, but Harry holds the key to keeping Justin and Betty safe."

Harry returned her gaze but said nothing. If he had guessed what she was about to say, his expression didn't show it.

"I'm asking Harry to make sure that his people are always on hand. I don't want them being too obtrusive but you saw the guys out front. No one is getting past them in a hurry."

Everyone looked at Harry, who nodded once. "I trust your instincts, Martha, but I also think you are wise to take every precaution. I'll have the people we need here at all times."

Martha was grateful to Harry for not making a big thing of it. He'd said yes and that was it. She looked at Justin, who smiled his approval.

"That's all great. I'll leave you guys to make what plans you need to."

CHAPTER 19

Harry clapped his hands together and said, "What's Plan B?"

Martha drew a deep breath. "This is completely left field but what about planting listening bugs in Green's cars? He and his team must be getting around London somehow."

The response was immediate and negative. Her team didn't like what they were hearing and they weren't afraid to say so. It was Julie's voice that came to the fore.

"I don't think that will work at all. My bet is we won't get near the vehicles, and even if by some miracle we managed to place a tracker somewhere, they're bound to pick it up in a security sweep. Some things are obvious, and sweeping your car for bugging devices is right up there. At least it is for people like this." The huge woman shook her head. "Sorry Martha, but that plan's a non-starter."

"I agree with Julie," said Justin. "Normally I'm right behind you but this time I think you may need to come up with Plan C. Sorry, Martha." He grimaced.

Harry said nothing. He was thinking about the car with the blacked-out windows that had been spotted outside of Betty's school.

"Actually," said Martha, spreading her arms wide. "I was thinking we bug the drivers."

"Now you really are losing the plot," said Julie. "If we'd have trouble bugging the cars, bugging the drivers would be harder. What are you proposing, that we distract them and plant a bug on their clothing?" Her incredulous expression said more than her words. "Like Justin said, it's a non-starter. And where are we going to get these bugs from?"

"Okay, okay," Martha held her hands up. "I'm stringing you along a bit. I'm thinking that we aim to bug the driver's homes. Not the person. I doubt that would be covered by any routine sweeps and it could provide what we need."

Two of her audience were still looking sceptical but Harry seemed interested. Martha knew she needed to crack on before she got on everyone's nerves.

"I'm willing to bet that at least one driver wants out from what they're doing. A year ago these guys were doing their jobs, no pressure, no threats, and thinking life was just grand. Of course, they would have been warned to be careful but basically they were being well paid to drive around in nice cars.

"Fast forward to today and they've been sucked into something altogether more sinister. And there's no way out. Saying they want to quit will earn them a bullet in the head, so they're stuck where they are.

"At work they'll be super cautious about what they say and who they say it to, but in their own homes they're bound to feel much more relaxed. If we can listen in to some conversations, we should be able to identify someone who is desperate to get out of Green's nasty little operation. Someone who we can persuade there is a way out. If we can find the right person I think they will jump at the chance to leave."

She paused. "Look, I know this needs a lot more thought to work but what if we make them an offer? They do a bit of spying for us, we offer them a new life under the witness protection scheme. How does that sound?"

"You might just have something there," said Harry. "It could work. I presume you want me to get a man on the inside to identify who these drivers are? And then what?

Follow them to find out where they live?" He frowned. "I do have one immediate thought, and this is based on your warning that we don't know who our enemies are. We should assume that we won't be able to rely on the police, at least not in the beginning. I could see them being taken off for witness protection and never being seen again. It might be best if we look after them ourselves, at least until we know it is safe to hand them over. I assume you'd like me to plan this bit."

"You got it in one, Harry," said Martha. "As you say, I'm also hoping you can provide all the people with the skill sets we'll need."

"I should be able to do that . . . hopefully," said Harry.

"Don't tell me," said Julie. "You've got a bloke who knows another bloke who can lend you some surveillance experts?"

"Almost right. It's actually a woman who knows a bloke with the right people."

"I've said it before, Harry," said Martha. "But you really are remarkable."

"Pleased to help, ma'am." He tapped his forehead in a mock salute.

"Well, thanks again," said Martha. "Now I've got one more question. And this is for all of you. What do I tell the Commissioner?"

CHAPTER 20

The question briefly hung in the air then Julie waved a languid hand. "You've already made your mind up, haven't you, Martha? So, what you're really asking is will Harry, Justin and I talk you out of it?"

A puzzled expression flitted across Justin's face and Julie winked at him. "She wants to keep the Commissioner well out of it and she wants us to agree with her." She poked Harry in the ribs. The big woman did not possess a light touch. Harry didn't flinch. She went on. "I can't speak for the elderly geezer but I would be very surprised if he didn't share my view that the less you tell the Old Bill, the better. Present company excepted, of course," she added, bowing in the direction of Martha.

Harry laughed, a deep, smoky sound.

"You going to share your thoughts or are you going to chortle like some muscle-bound version of Buddha?" asked Julie.

Harry looked suitably inscrutable.

"Come on, baldie. Tell us what you think," Julie persisted.

"I was waiting for Justin. It's called being polite and letting other people have a say."

"Since when did you get polite?" said Julie, before adding with a theatrical sigh, "I suppose there's a first time for everything."

"Actually, I did want to say something," said Justin. "I think we bug the drivers but we don't tell the police. What you're planning is illegal and there's no way the Commissioner could back the plan. But it's a good idea and might give us what we need."

"I agree with Justin." Harry winked at Julie, who shrugged. "You know what I think . . . keep the bugging to ourselves."

"So, we're all in agreement," said Martha. "I didn't think it would be that easy, but good. Now — since we're all probably hungry — let's order pizza and we can work on the details. Anyone know what they want or do you need a menu?"

"Make mine a double pepperoni with extra chilli," said Harry.

"Me too," chorused Julie and Justin.

"So, no one going for the vegan option?" said Martha.

"I'm eating less meat all the time, but tonight I need something a bit chunkier," replied Julie.

"Right, this is my treat," said Martha. "I know that we have decided to abstain while this is going on, but I don't think one bottle of lager is going to do us any harm." She reached into the fridge and extracted four ice-cold bottles.

Julie dished out the drinks and there was a brief and appreciative silence while everyone enjoyed their first sip of cold lager.

Martha put her bottle down. "Right, let's focus on the plan. I want to really think things through. I know we've all agreed, in principle, but if anyone spots a flaw once we get into the nitty gritty then please shout out. If this goes wrong and we end up in trouble with the Commissioner, well, I don't like to think about the consequences.

"I'm not trying to big this up, but I've come to the conclusion that there are people at the very highest levels of Scotland Yard who would just love it if I fell on my face. They'd be like sharks scenting blood in the water. It would let them discredit me as much as they liked."

"I haven't been looking at things that way," said Justin, his forehead creasing in anger. "But now you raise it, I see exactly what you mean. Do you have any handle on the scale of the threat in terms of numbers of officers or their seniority?"

"I'm afraid it could be the Commissioner herself," said Martha.

Justin looked even more anxious. "How sure are you?"

"I can't be totally sure but I have been giving it a lot of thought. And why not Paula Charteris? Tony Green could have picked her out years ago, when she was setting out before she hit the fast track. He might have been keeping her under wraps in the hope she got to the top."

"But no one could have been totally sure she was going to be made a commissioner," objected Justin.

"No, you're right," said Martha. "But over the years a lot of people have said she stood out so she was in with a shout from quite early on. And we know that Green is a calculating bastard. He might have decided she was worth a punt. Money's not an issue for him. One more on the pay roll won't hurt. And even if it's not Paula herself, what about her office? She has all sorts of officers attached to her team." Martha tapped her finger on the table. "There's even some of those lovely people from MI5 there. All of them listening in and knowing stuff long before anyone else does."

"You make a convincing case," said Justin. "I'm glad I agreed with your plan to keep the Commissioner out of our business."

"You're asking the right questions," said a suddenly sombre Harry. "We do know there are people who would love to cause trouble for Martha. And I mean real trouble — like the time they tried to hurt her in prison."

Julie picked up the mood. "Ever since she unmasked Tony Green, Martha has been promised that an elite team of officers is on the case and she has nothing to worry about. Well, I don't see any elite protection cops sitting in here. My gut says we stay wary to stay safe."

Harry had listened intently while Martha spoke, his mood a mixture of apprehension over what the future held and pride at the clear-sighted and tough woman she had become.

"I think I can safely say that we're all in this with you," he said. He raised his bottle in silent salute, which was matched by the other three.

"Thank you for that," Martha said. "Now, can we get on before you make me cry."

Julie grinned and playfully punched Martha in the arm, making her wince.

"Who's going to initiate the bugging plan?" said Martha, trying not to rub her upper arm — that "friendly tap" had brought tears to her eyes. She was going to have a bruise.

CHAPTER 21

The underground compound was enormous. Corridor after corridor leading to room after room. And Tony Green was the only person in it. Which made him nervous, a thought he only admitted to because he was alone. It was one of his golden rules: Never ever let your underlings see your fear.

But as he walked down yet another empty corridor, with closed doors on both sides, it was easy to let his imagination run away with him. Deadly enemies could be hiding anywhere. The fear factor was amplified by the oppressive silence. Even the air-conditioning system emitted a barely discernible hum. The only other noise was his ragged breathing and the gentle pad of his feet as he moved through the space, brilliantly lit with multiple ceiling lights. Opening each door, Tony Green couldn't help holding his breath until he was sure no one was lurking inside.

Not only was his search proving unnerving, it was taking far longer than he had anticipated since the space had turned out to be bigger and more complex than he had imagined, a great deal more complicated.

It took time before he was confident enough that he had a sense of how it all fitted together. Not that Tony Green would trust his own senses — he was also going to involve someone with the expertise to map out everything in proper detail. Getting that right was going to be crucial to both keeping him safe and allowing him to wrap up his UK operation. There was something about this space that made it easy to get turned around and he was not a man who could tolerate getting caught because he'd taken the wrong turning. He was adamant — nothing got left to chance. He'd spent enough time on his own, now he needed his hand-picked crew to pull it all together. He had the beginning of a plan and a cup of coffee would be just the thing to help him make the final choices.

He made his way back to the main kitchen area, which took longer than it should have because he took a wrong turn, something he attributed to allowing himself to get distracted by thoughts of murdering Martha. It kept happening and needed to stop. First things first, coffee, then get his people in here and get them to work.

The burst of stress made his cheek bones start to feel hot and tight. Even though he knew there was nothing to it, he hated the sensation. It made him imagine his cheeks were bright red — making him stand out like he was waving his arms and shouting, "Look at me." Perhaps he'd been a little hasty in getting rid of the surgeon and his team. Now he had no one to take advice from.

Filling up a kettle, he shrugged. What was done was done. There could be no possibility of going back and he was never going to ask for a second opinion. To be fair, the surgeon had warned him it would happen and everyone assured him he didn't look like his cheek bones were glowing red. He made himself change gear mentally. There was no point repeatedly going over old ground. It would get him nowhere and just took up valuable thinking space.

He put the kettle on and looked around. There was a serious-looking coffee machine sitting prominently in the kitchen but he didn't spare it a second glance. He preferred instant. Life was too short to make your own cappuccino.

This space was the first place he'd found and the last he'd left to check. He was aware of a low noise, slightly deeper than the one he'd locked on to as being temperature control. Perhaps a sophisticated air extraction system? One designed to eliminate all odours? He made a note that he needed to make sure he got that checked out. He didn't want to get caught out by the smell of a bacon sandwich. He was sure the creators of this amazing space would have considered that but it never hurt to check.

The place was set up like a small canteen with a big table surrounded by a dozen chairs and banks of electrical goods including fridges, freezers, ovens, microwaves and air fryers. Like all the equipment down here, it was made by the most expensive brands, the sort that took serious money to buy, especially in these quantities. He'd been wondering what they did if something was faulty until he discovered a space crammed full of replacements still in their packaging. He again silently thanked the creator of this space, of whom he was going to be the unintended, but very grateful, beneficiary.

Pouring hot water over his instant coffee, he wondered how long the supplies would last. Quite a time, maybe three weeks for twelve people. It was more than enough. He had no intention of holing up here for any prolonged period. But that didn't mean there was no point in pursuing some interesting new lines that had emerged from John Munro's other book. There were some extremely influential and wealthy people identified in that. And none of them would want their secrets exposed. For the right price, he could keep it that way. Doing deals wherever he could was something that was in his blood.

He was very good at the dark arts of his business, never thinking twice as he ordered the death of a victim. But that was the kind of thing that mostly required brute force. What really got him going was the chance to use his brain and outwit an opponent, getting one over on somebody — no matter how small the deal — was what really motivated him and got him out of bed in the morning. To his intense irritation, this line of reasoning led Tony Green to start thinking about Martha again, since there could be no escaping the fact that she and her minions had outwitted him.

He shook his head angrily. *Stop it*, he told himself. *Get on with your work.*

Tony Green had decided to pick the first three names in John Munro's second book. A Chinese businessman, a good contact, had once told him that three was a lucky number. He decided to test that now.

The three names jumped out at him. They were in a league of their own, and would be just perfect. As he read their names, the thought occurred that if he pulled this off it was likely he would be behind one of the most successful blackmail attempts ever.

It would take a bit of extra effort but the rewards would be very lucrative indeed. And to the small number of people who understood exactly what he did, it would cement his place in the history of crime. It would be a fitting legacy — something he thoroughly deserved. Even if he thought so himself.

It was time to start placing some phone calls and reminding people that they had a new master. One they needed to be respectful of if they intended to keep the public ignorant about their real selves, cynical chancers who squirrelled away public money and hid it where they thought nobody else knew about it . . . That might indeed have been the case, had Tony Green not been able to spend time with the Banker. Now Tony knew all their secrets — and exactly how to use them in order to profit himself.

He picked up his phone and tapped in the number for the first name on his list. It was answered quickly, as it was his target's personal telephone. The voice on the other end would have sounded very familiar to many people within Parliament.

The voice sounded cool and confident. Used to command. Green intended to do something about that.

"I do not intend to repeat myself and how you respond will determine how you survive this encounter," he said.

"Who is this? How did you get this number?"

"Two very good questions, which I'm about to answer. So, like I already said, listen very carefully. This is the last time I will ever repeat myself in a conversation with you and you don't want to know what happens if you make me try to change that rule."

Green had always been good at reading other people and, even in those few seconds of conversation, he had noted that a slight sense of doubt had crept in to undermine the confidence of the person he'd called.

Green started talking. His instructions were precise.

CHAPTER 22

Martha was one of those people who really hated being late, so much so that she invariably turned up a good twenty minutes early, happy to wait, secure in the knowledge that whatever else happened she would be on time. This morning she was paying the price for this habit having sat outside Paula Charteris's office for almost an hour — a third of that self-imposed.

To be fair, they had given her a comfortable seat in a small waiting area just off the anteroom of the Commissioner's office. The anteroom had four uniformed officers sitting at desks and the area was a hive of activity, with people coming and going, phones ringing and an apparently endless flow of digital messages being dealt with. She gained the impression that most of the messages were moved on pretty quickly to the relevant team. The Commissioner hadn't got where she was by allowing urgent inquiries to die a lingering death hanging around her in-tray.

On arrival, an inspector had guided her to the waiting area. It was a functional space with minimal decoration. A large picture on one of the walls showed the late Queen Elizabeth, pinning something to the Commissioner's formal dress uniform. Both women were smiling broadly.

The inspector who had guided her in was also all smiles and seemed genuinely interested in Martha. She offered her a tea or coffee, which Martha declined on the grounds she was still buzzing from drinking one of Harry's extra strong teas, which contained at least a day's worth of caffeine. She was now wishing she'd said yes. If nothing else, drinking it would have been something to do.

For a while, she admired the view across London from the top of the New Scotland Yard building. At one point, a window cleaner with all the safety gear had appeared and started washing the windows. The inspector reappeared and noted her gaze. "Even the window cleaners are fully security-checked around here. You can't have just anybody gazing in to see what you're up to."

"I did wonder," said Martha.

Towards the end of her vigil, a man and woman in civilian clothes had waited with her but had brusquely rebuffed her attempt at communication. Instead, they sat as far away as the space would allow and whispered to each other, never once sparing her a second glance. Infuriatingly, they had gulped down all the water from two large bottles left out on a table in the centre of the room.

The final insult came when they were called away after a short ten-minute delay. As she left, the woman gave her a look of transparently insincere sympathy and said, "Sorry, we seem to have jumped the queue." Martha's arm twitched as she resisted the urge to give the woman the finger. There was something about her that was familiar but she couldn't quite place her face or her name. She was quite sure she had never seen the man before. As they left, she consoled herself with the hope that all that water would soon be having a keen impact on the woman's bladder.

Twenty more minutes dragged by before Martha was finally called in. The Commissioner was waiting just outside her door to greet her. In pictures, she always looked immaculate, an impression reinforced in person. She was nearly as tall as Martha, possibly a little broader and boasted prominent cheek bones and a smile that touched her hazel-coloured eyes as she offered her hand.

Martha never liked to read too much into these things, especially with people she had only just met, but could feel that there was a sense of tension drifting off the woman, and she wondered what was causing it. Then again, this was the Commissioner of the Metropolitan Police and she would have plenty on her plate.

"Come in, Martha. Come in." If a voice could sound efficient, then this one was very efficient indeed.

Paula Charteris led the way into her inner office, furnished quite simply. Practical rather than stylish. This was somebody who was sending a clear signal — I put functionality ahead of comfort because I'm here to do a job.

Ordinarily, Martha might have observed the few personal touches, the family pictures in frames on the desk and a montage devoted to newspaper headlines and cartoons put together when she was made Commissioner two years ago. It wasn't much, but at least it added a slight human touch.

But Martha wasn't paying attention to any of that. She wouldn't even have taken a second look if the Commissioner had put up a picture of herself in a bathing suit — her eyes were firmly on the couple who had gone in ahead of her. She had not anticipated that either of these two would be present for her meeting. She had assumed that this would be a one-to-one encounter. How wrong she was.

The pair were sitting at a round table, big enough for ten people at least. The man was gazing at a point between his feet. He was so still he might have been turned to stone. The woman, meanwhile, was holding her right arm out in front of her face, studying her red-painted nails. Pointedly, neither acknowledged her. It was a clear statement of one-upmanship. Martha decided she could play this game and turned back to Paula Charteris with a bright smile.

The Commissioner did a great job of ignoring the atmosphere in the room. She guided Martha over to the table and indicated she take a seat to the right of a small, neat pile of documents, seating herself to the left.

"Sorry you had to wait, Martha, but I hope what you're about to hear will make it worthwhile. Just to remind you, please don't take any notes or discuss these matters with unauthorised third parties." There was a short pause then she quickly carried on. "First of all, the bad news. We still haven't got Green or have any credible information about where he is. We've had various suggestions but none has checked out. We did get a vague suggestion that he has changed his appearance, but we couldn't get anything more, and our informant has now disappeared."

Martha showed no reaction to this news but internally she logged it for later discussion with Harry, Julie and Justin. It was interesting that the Commissioner had revealed Scotland Yard investigators had found this information out. In fact, she was quite surprised that the Yard team wasn't actively pursuing more information.

If that sounded harsh, she thought, then they should just try living her life of the past few years. Not only that, but the two strangers were distinctly unfriendly. She was going to be very careful to keep her guard up at all times and not just when she was in meetings like this.

"I do have some better news for you," the Commissioner's words broke into her chain of thought. "Given the extreme sensitivity of this case we are putting together a joint operation between the Counterterrorism Command, the Anti-Corruption Command and MI5. The commander of this new team will report directly to me. I believe Tony Green's activities amount to a threat to national security and we need to take it seriously."

She took a sip of water then turned to Martha. "I have personally insisted that you are part of this team. It is only thanks to you that we know about this man and we now also know he was behind your mother's murder, the kidnap of your child and attempts on your life. If anyone deserves the chance to help bring this man to justice, it's you." She thumped her hand on the table and looked at the pair seated together. "This is an MI5-led operation so they have the final say. I wish I had time to stay but I have to be somewhere else, so I am going to leave the three of you to talk." With that she walked out, leaving Martha to wonder what her role was going to be as part of this new team.

She nodded at the other two and put on her brightest smile. "A wild guess . . . but you two are MI5? I'm Martha Munro, but you already know that."

In reply they said nothing, just got up and walked to the door. The man walked straight out without a backward glance. Flabbergasted, Martha watched the woman pause in the doorway then turn sharply to face her.

"I was always told you judge someone by their friends. Well, we've looked at your friends and we don't like what we see. If you're expecting any kind of role on the new team you can think again. It's only because of the Commissioner you are here at all. But let me be crystal clear — we don't like you, we don't trust you, and that goes for your friends too."

She marched out, leaving Martha staring open-mouthed at the door. She had no idea what to do — these were the people she was supposed to be working with, yet she didn't have any idea where this new team was based or what her role was supposed to be.

She didn't even have the name of the woman and her underling, as she had dubbed the man.

Her introspection was interrupted when one of the Commissioner's aides stuck his head round the door. He was a superintendent she recognised from previous visits.

"Come with me, Martha," said the officer. "You look like someone with questions. I'll do what I can to fill in the gaps but Paula said to tell you — and this is strictly off the record — that you're going to find things difficult."

As she followed him, she was glad that he couldn't see the incredulous expression that was plastered on her face. She knew Scotland Yard was not a place for the faint-hearted, given that it was full of ambitious people wanting to get on and grab the reins of power for themselves. But this surely took the biscuit.

Her face darkened with anger and she promised herself that whatever else happened she would not be intimidated.

I'm not scared of anyone here, she thought. *Whatever else you've got up your sleeves — bring it on.*

CHAPTER 23

The superintendent led her to an office a short walk away. Martha followed him inside and ignored the view of London. She wasn't in the mood for scenery — she wanted facts, and hopefully was about to get some. The officer took a seat at a long wooden table and indicated she sit near to him but not so close she was in his personal space.

"Paul Wrench," he told her, offering his hand. He was a big man with powerful shoulders and gave off a sense of calm competence, which acted as a balm to Martha's wounded feelings. Sometimes she was happy to rely on her instincts. And on this occasion, her instincts were telling her that this was a man that she could trust, at least up to a point.

He looked at her steadily for a few seconds, long enough to make sure he had her close attention. "You're not going to like what I tell you," he said, "but you would do well to reflect on it for a little while. Give yourself the time to make a decision that's right for you, Martha."

She made to reply, leaning forward and taking a breath, then sat back and waited. The words that had begun forming in her brain were left in place. She would listen to what this man said. And think about her response before anything else. It was a lesson that had been drummed into her by Harry many times over the years. Sometimes silence is your best friend. Let the other person do all the talking. You do all the listening. It was surprising how much information people were prepared to give you if you didn't keep filling the silence with questions.

Wrench nodded in acknowledgement and she thought a slight twinkle brightened his pale blue eyes. For just a moment, she had the clear sense that he was reading her like a book. While she had already decided that she could trust this man, she would also have to be careful not to be too trusting.

"I heard you were a quick study, Martha. Well done, you're going to need that. Before I tell you more, let me say this: . You have some powerful friends who are keeping a close watch on developments."

From somewhere he produced a small hip flask. Now there was no doubt about the twinkle in his eye. "First, a drink, then get to it?" He waggled the flask gently in the air.

Martha waved off the offer with a polite smile. She was determined not to let her feelings show but she was concerned. If you were being given the good news first, followed by a drink, then the bad news was likely to be pretty bad. If that was the case she wanted to meet it stone-cold sober. She didn't know much about Wrench other than he was a rising star who had won promotion while working with the anti-terror team and was regarded as ambitious and clever. But she knew it would be foolish to assume this man was on anybody's side but his own.

If he'd noticed her short bout of introspection, it didn't show and he put away the hip flask with a brief, "This can be our little secret."

Martha, who by now was firing on all cylinders, wondered for a moment if the whole drink thing had been a brilliant move to lure her into a conspiracy because it was a shared moment of secrecy. Then she shook herself. She was reading too much into what was going on. He'd offered a drink, she'd refused. The end.

Meanwhile, Wrench, who had taken a quick look out of the window, turned his gaze back towards her. "There's no easy way to put this, Martha, so I'll say my bit, then you can ask questions."

Her stomach turned acidic. She was glad to have skipped breakfast this morning otherwise she would have been nauseous.

"A few moments ago, I said you had some powerful friends," said Wrench. "Well, that comes with a bit of an add-on. You also have some powerful enemies. There are people here who don't like you."

There it was — the killer line. Not just that she had enemies. That wasn't a surprise. Not at all. What was alarming was the confirmation that her enemies still had the confidence to reach out and try to hurt her, even here in the heart of Scotland Yard. It brought into sharp focus all those fears about the safety of her family and friends. If they felt bold enough to take on Martha, a serving police officer under the protection of the Commissioner — at least, she hoped that was the case — what else might they do?

Martha felt angry and disappointed at the same time. She felt like she did after one of those boxing sessions with Harry when he caught her with a series of rapid-fire jabs to the body. Individually, there was no knockout punch but the cumulative effect hurt. It was like a lot of Harry's lessons. They often seemed to hurt before they eventually made sense and offered insights that were hard to ignore. This particular one was filed under, "There's never such a thing as a friendly fight!"

Carefully controlling her breathing and feeling her heartbeat slow down, she started asking herself difficult questions, like: What if she was right that the Commissioner was her biggest enemy? She certainly had the power to make her life unpleasant.

Martha almost spoke aloud in frustration. She kept going down this path — how could she possibly know if she could trust Paula Charteris? On the basis of what had happened so far today, she could place no trust in her at all. But maybe what she was about to hear would change all that.

Wrench was looking at her very closely again. She got the strongest impression that he was asking himself the same questions about her that she was asking about him. Getting those answers right might prove the hardest thing she had to do. But she also sensed that now was not the time to push. She needed to go away, think about what she'd been told and talk to Harry and Julie, see what they made of it and come up with a new plan, which was easy in theory.

The superintendent stared at the door. The message seemed clear. It was time to go. She got up, nodded once and stepped out of the meeting room.

CHAPTER 24

Her mind was already turning to catching up with Harry, Julie and Justin — this morning had been a washout on many levels, but there were a few nuggets worth going over with the team.

Absorbed in her thoughts, it took her a moment to realise that Wrench was calling to her . . . not just talking to her, but calling her back. She stopped and turned to see him in the doorway.

"Sorry, I wasn't sending you away, although I can see how me staring at the door might have given you the idea I was. Actually, I was thinking I should check the door in case anyone was listening outside . . . so while you're there, anyone dodgy in sight?"

The area was clear and Martha shook her head, resisting the urge to smile. There might be a touch of cloak and dagger about this, but she didn't want to get too pally with someone she'd literally just met. Wrench was one of those people who could make you feel like a friend after a few minutes. But as tempting as it was to let her guard down, she resisted. He might be on her side, he might not. That didn't matter for the moment. Right now, she needed to listen carefully to anything he might have to say.

Wrench was looking at her with a concerned expression that seemed genuine, but how could she really tell? She was in danger of losing control and desperate for answers to the questions that were piling up everywhere she turned. An image of Harry came to mind and she knew what to do. She was right to be cautious but needed to keep her sense of perspective. While her encounters this morning would have been enough to put anyone on edge, she had to get more information before deciding who was a friend and who was an enemy. There was trouble coming for sure, but as Harry always said, "If you go looking for bother, you'll find it."

All of a sudden, she smiled. She knew the answer — go with the flow, get all the information she could and then back home to the people she could really trust. Decision made, her mind seemed to slow down, allowing her to gather her thoughts. Her brain had been throwing out so many scenarios she couldn't keep up with the ideas.

"Are you okay to crack on?" asked Wrench.

"I'm fine, thank you, sir." Martha had moved back into the room. "Just trying to get some sense of what you're telling me. And I do have some questions, if that's okay?"

"Fire away," said Wrench. "Although I wouldn't say no to a drink of water. There's a small fridge in the corner."

He got up and took out two bottles, bringing them back to their seats. An odd thought popped into her head — an ancient Japanese saying: *In the house of your enemies never drink the tea.*

Okay. She had just made that up, but she felt it worked well in the circumstances. She knew what it meant.

"My first and obvious question," said Martha. "Who wants to derail me?"

Wrench swallowed some water and shrugged apologetically. "Sorry, that bit is well above my pay grade. I don't normally pass on information unless I can at least question the source, but the Commissioner said it was important you knew how dangerous your enemies are and you need to be on your toes."

"I bet she did," said Martha, this latest bit of information adding to the idea that the Commissioner needed to be closely watched. As before, she was careful to hold her emotions in check — it wouldn't do to offer any insights to her enemies. And that might well include Paul Wrench. Much as it pained her to even think it. She genuinely liked this man.

"All right. Is there anything else that you can tell me?" asked Martha. "Maybe you have a bit of background detail?"

He shrugged again. "Not much for you, except I think that something changed in the last week or so. But there is a sense that the dynamics have shifted, and very recently. There is one other thing, and I'm sorry but I'm not entirely sure of this, but the people who are after you may not just be police officers."

Martha's mouth opened to ask a question, but Wrench waved his hand gently. "Sorry, Martha, like I said, I don't know for sure."

Not much, but at least something. Martha suspected he didn't have a great deal more to offer but she was going to push this as far as she could. She had to make the most of any opportunity to pick up scraps of information. It saddened her but nothing she was hearing now suggested she was wrong to place so much trust in her friends and so little in her police colleagues.

Without really thinking about it, Martha found herself moving into interrogation mode. Which didn't get her very far. She kept running into a version of "no comment," or, as Wrench put it, "Sorry, I don't have that information." What she needed was to find something he could freely talk about while also winning his confidence. And she needed to be careful about not insulting his intelligence and losing him as a potential ally.

Thinking on her feet, she decided the safest approach was to tackle the issue of MI5, since she knew many senior police officers had reservations about the way the organisation operated. "Spooks" was how her father had referred to them, and he hadn't meant it in a complimentary way. With a bit of luck, Wrench would also think of MI5 as being a shady bunch of characters not held to the same standards as the Met itself. If she was really lucky, he'd privately share her view that policing was for the police and national security was for the spooks. It might just give them something they had in common. Not quite a bond, but close to it.

She needed to crack on, although looking at his calm demeanour, it seemed that her internal debate had not caused him any concern.

"Can you tell me any more about this task force that's been set up?" asked Martha. "How usual is it to get MI5 involved? If MI5 is running it, where does that leave the police? What's the overall remit?"

"Want to add any more to that? I counted at least four questions there. Maybe five," said Wrench, smiling to show it wasn't a criticism.

"No, that will do," Martha replied, smiling back to show she understood. Mentally, she had her fingers firmly crossed. All of Wrench's body language indicated that he was ready to part with a little extra of what he knew. If only she could just find a way of persuading him that she was worth his while taking a risk on.

"Okay," said Wrench. He seemed to have come to some sort of conclusion and leaned forward. "Let me try to fill you in. At least as much as I'm able to. There's always been quite a bit of information shared between ourselves and MI5. That has become more widespread in recent years as the country faces more threats, especially from terrorism or hacking attempts on our most sensitive infrastructure."

He underlined this point by spreading his hands wide as if underlining the scale of the problems.

"As you may be aware," he went on, "relations between ourselves and the denizens of Thames House have not always been at their best, a combination, I think, of suspicion and ignorance. Things are better now thanks to more regular contact, at least at command level." He stopped to rub his nose with a tissue taken from his pocket.

Martha could not tell if Wrench thought this new closeness was a good thing or not, and before she could decide he was talking again.

"Sorry for what must sound like a history lesson, but the point is that this idea, for a joint task force, came from their side at one of these meetings, although it was no spur-of-the-moment thing. I'm told it was presented as a done deal with support from GCHQ and the Cabinet Office. In other words, we were informed and told it was their idea so they ran it."

Martha coughed lightly to cover a smile. She'd spotted that Wrench had clenched and unclenched his hands while he was talking. He was clearly not impressed by the way the security services had behaved. But then this was hardly news as far as the police were concerned. His next comment gave Martha a little more information. And some insight into the way Scotland Yard had reacted to the news that MI5 wanted to run a special ops team.

"Rather than fight it," he went on, his expression giving away nothing about how he truly felt about this, "the Commissioner took the pragmatic view that it was best to play along. She nominated you to be part of it. That's why you were asked here today. This all happened very fast. In the last forty-eight hours. So, I don't think anybody has really got their heads round exactly how this is going to work and, more importantly, from your point of view, how it will affect what we do as we look further ahead."

He looked at Martha, who was glaring at him. "You want to know what this means for you?"

She very slightly inclined her head. Inside, she was screaming to say something more. Ask some more questions. But she kept her cool, remembering Harry's sound words of advice — and his painful trick of hitting her with a cluster of lightweight punches in boxing training when she wasn't paying attention.

"Politics is what happens now. The boss anticipated this might happen and decided ahead of time that she wouldn't back down. As far as she's concerned you're in and they have to lump it. I know this must make you feel like the little piggy in the middle. The best news is that this doesn't guarantee you get asked aboard — but, this way, it forces MI5 to declare their hand, rather than trying to fudge the issue and making out it was all to do with us. Which is just typical of them to be honest, always thinking ahead about who will get the blame if something goes wrong and there needs to be an investigation.

"Don't get me wrong. The police can be just as bad about arse covering as anyone. But at least we try to get the operation done first and worry about what went wrong afterwards. Personally, I hate it when I encounter people whose first position is damage limitation before anything's even happened!" He stopped speaking and carefully placed his hands on the desk in front of him, clearly an attempt to calm himself down. Martha was still glaring. They both knew that he had still left her dangling about what was happening. But at least he had now given her some context to work with and an indication that he was closer to her line of thinking than she had first thought. She still had questions, lots and lots of questions. But she massively appreciated the apparent show of support he had just provided by letting her in on some of the backroom secrets.

It was a start.

Maybe this man could become an ally and a trusted source.

Time would tell . . . but that was the one thing she knew she was short of.

While these thoughts were running around her head, Wrench had clearly been waiting for an opportunity to finish his conversation.

"We can't get away from the fact that you turned over the proverbial hornets' nest when you unmasked that bastard Tony Green," he said. "We're all guilty by association and that allows MI5 to claim that not one of us can be trusted. You especially, because you were closer to the conspiracy than most. And those doubts will remain in place until everybody's name is properly cleared.

"You may find what I say next incredible." He sighed, an exasperated sound. "There are voices, influential voices, who say you might be part of a plot, a plot designed to discredit the Met by using you as a Trojan horse. They keep saying that every time something goes wrong you are close by — right at the centre of events. Frankly, it's a ludicrous idea, as anybody taking just a moment to think about it could work out for themselves. But like I said, these are strange times and people tend to believe what they want to believe."

He frowned, making him look tired. "Step carefully, Martha. These are difficult times at the Met. People are looking over their shoulders and wondering who the enemy is. At the same time, many people are seeing this as an opportunity to grab power for themselves and move ahead of their rivals. It really is a mess just now, and not one that a novice should be wandering around in. That's not to say you aren't capable of getting through this on your own. You've more than proved that on several occasions. But I've never known anything like it. You really can't trust anybody, not unless you know them thoroughly."

Martha clamped her teeth so tight she almost forgot to breathe. She really wanted to punch someone but she needed to regain control. It was idiotic to think that she might be some form of Trojan horse. As if! This was a classic "blame the victim" moment and she suspected it didn't help that she was a woman — it probably was contributing factor for those pouring the poison. What was coming next, she wondered?

Wrench could have been mind-reading. "I know, I know. The whole idea is utterly ludicrous. And I really don't know where it has come from, but it has thrown a spanner in the works. The boss says you might want to take a few days off? Out of sight and out of mind is the theory, but I very much doubt you want to do anything like that. You strike me as the sort of woman who will go out there and find answers to her questions."

That, thought Martha, *is exactly what I want*. If Wrench was up for it. She had a few more questions. Then she needed to get home to the security of her own team, and they could decipher exactly what Wrench had told her. Because she was quite certain somewhere in all that had been said there were some important clues or pointers that were going to help her progress.

Wrench stood up. It was clearly time to call it a day, at least as far as he was concerned. She didn't try to persuade him otherwise. She knew he had gone out on a limb for her, even though she still had questions. Now it was important that she demonstrated that she understood how the game was meant to be played and didn't try to force him into saying things he didn't want to. Not that that was likely. He was far too tough for that kind of thing.

A handshake later and she was waiting for the lift to take her back to the ground floor. She decided to walk back to Victoria railway station. It would do her good to get some fresh air before taking the train home. She had started to feel a suffocating sense of being trapped.

Walking away from the building, she wondered what was going to happen next. With so many senior officers seemingly stabbing one another in the back, she wondered what she was going to face next. This might be a confusing mess but she was convinced of one thing: Tony Green was playing an active part in sowing discord, which meant he couldn't be far away.

Holding that thought, she sent a text to Harry. *Get the kettle on . . . lots to discuss.*

CHAPTER 25

As he sank back against the luxurious leather seats of the Mercedes S-class, Tony Green's driver pointed out the small package on the back seat.

"The courier dropped this at my house first thing this morning, sir."

Green nodded to show he'd heard and carefully reached for the parcel. He pulled out a burner phone preloaded with one telephone number.

"Any message?" said Green, gazing out of the tinted rear window at the crowded pavement outside Harrods. He loved the S-class, stuffed with technology and perfect climate control that kept the interior effortlessly cool. But its best feature? In London, it just blended in. Its black paintwork made it one among many, especially over in the West End.

"Yes, sir," said the driver. "I was told to tell you to expect contact at either twelve noon or 2 p.m."

Green blinked slowly. This was good news. It opened the possibility that he was going to get an update on the loathsome Martha. Feeling he was about to go off on a fantasy where he extracted painful revenge for her ruining his life, he distracted himself by checking the weather. Good — it was still dry and mild, good walking conditions.

With the car heading east, they glided slowly past the Royal Albert Hall. "This will do," he told the driver. He could double-back on foot into Hyde Park, then Kensington Gardens and make his way to the ever-busy Kensington High Street. If today's telephone call came through, he intended to use that as the starting point for his fightback.

He had plenty of time before he needed to be at what he hoped would be his new HQ. Once he moved his people in, he would give himself three weeks to save what he could of his empire and strike back against Martha and her odious side-kicks, that deranged pensioner Harry and the oversized Julie.

Taking a convoluted route, he arrived at his destination with forty-five minutes to spare and was in the kitchen finishing a cup of coffee when the burner rang. He picked up immediately. "Report."

"She's just left Scotland Yard."

"I need to know more about how she reacted to the meeting." Green paused and listened to the steady breathing of the person on the end of the phone. The cardinal rule was to never use names and he wasn't about to start now. There was no change in the breathing, which pleased him. The nervous ones always let themselves down with ragged, rapid breaths as the tension stretched their nerves. He didn't mind them being scared of him, but not controlling fear made you error-prone, which could lead to disaster.

"She's a chip off the old block, that one. He had a great poker face and so does she." The contact stopped talking and Green waited patiently. Even now he was testing and prob-ing. He was reassured by the steady breathing he could hear on the other end of the line. There was no point in trying to rush her. She always measured her words and was an excellent judge of character. What she told him was worth waiting for. "As I said, you wouldn't want to play poker against her but just for a moment the mask slipped."

"What was it that made that happen?" Green was eager now and not hiding it very well. Anyone listening to his breathing would have heard it becoming sharper and shorter.

"It was being rebuffed by MI5 that caused it. It seemed to really shock her."

"Surely she must have thought that could happen?" said Green. "What made her react like that?"

"It wasn't just the being rebuffed that did her," replied the voice. "It was the way it was done. She was shot down in flames . . . told she could never be trusted. Your ideas about putting the mark on her really worked."

Green nodded but made no reply. He knew this contact never missed an opportunity to ingratiate herself and one of the ways she did that was by flattering the boss. Which only worked if you let it. He kept up the silent treatment until the woman spoke, her voice cracking with uncertainty.

"Are you there?"

A few more seconds of silence.

"No more arse-kissing." Green was gratified to hear the sudden intake of breath at the coarse language. "Talk me through exactly what happened."

The woman instantly started gabbling before catching herself. She was no fool and knew she was making a bad impression.

"Perhaps if we start again?" he suggested, this time keeping the irritation out of his voice. There weren't many people he would treat this carefully but she was in a key position and hadn't let him down in the past. He would give her the benefit of the doubt . . . at least for the time being.

Unaware of Green mentally debating her future, the woman had started on a detailed recount of everything she could recall from Martha's visit. She was careful to keep it short and sharp except when it came to the encounter with the MI5 pair.

"I didn't see it directly — only the three of them were in the boardroom when it happened, but I can provide some details.

"Martha had been left to stew in the waiting area, then the man and woman arrived. They sat as far away from Martha as they could. Then they were called in first, despite Martha having already waited.

"I saw the woman actually stop and lean close to Martha as she made some remark and whatever was said, the words obviously struck home because Martha had a face like thunder, and at first I thought she was going to stand up, maybe even confront her, but she got control pretty sharpish . . . although she was giving this woman the full laser-beam death stare as she walked out.

"The meeting between the agents and the Commissioner was very brief, then she left after calling Martha in. Once again it was very clear there were words spoken but I don't know by who.

"What I can say for sure is the MI5 woman instigated matters. She got halfway out of the door before turning round and going back inside. Whatever happened it was quick. The male agent had already left and the woman rapidly joined him. They didn't say anything, just got in the lift when it arrived.

"After that Martha and the superintendent went off to one of the side rooms. They were in there a few minutes, certainly long enough to exchange information, then Martha left. That's it really."

"What about these MI5 agents?" said Green. "What else can you tell me? Specifically, I'd like their names and what they were doing over there."

"I don't have much on that, I'm sorry to say. I don't know their names and there was no entry in the diary about their visit — which is a bit weird since the Commissioner gets steamed up if appointments aren't listed.

"I can make an informed guess, though. The Commissioner has been going on about setting up some joint task force between the police and MI5. She's been doing a bit of lobbying at the political level, trying to get some funding and officers assigned. I think this might have been about that."

"Okay," said Green. "Let me know if you think of anything else." He ended the call before she could respond. He needed to urgently think about something she'd just said.

Green wasn't a man given to introspection, looking into the past to see what could have been done better. He always took the view that life was what it was. But something in this conversation made him reflective and contemplate just what he had lost. He was far more than just a common criminal. He had been a CEO of Crime, the pilot of the ship, setting the course that others needed to follow.

All that had been taken from him. He knew he would never get it back. And that hurt more than he could say. He sighed loudly, the sound disappearing into the huge space. As much as he had been trying not to think too hard about Martha, perhaps there was little point in suppressing his feelings. Better to have them out in the open, where at least he had some control. Pushing them down too deep risked them disappearing then surfacing when he least expected them to.

He switched off the phone and made his way back out to street level. He would be returning to the mansion with his chief operating officer. If she approved the setup, they would stay the night and begin moving his key people in straight away.

He was about to leave when a sudden thought made him smile. Not many people could find a way of reaching out to the most senior people at Scotland Yard. MPs and PR men alike would give virtually anything to be able to boast the kind of contacts he possessed. Not bad for a fugitive who topped Scotland Yard's own most wanted list. It must have come as nasty surprise to Martha just how much power he still had and there was nothing she could do about it.

He rubbed his hands gleefully. Yes, he thought, Martha was a dead woman walking . . . and she was walking right into his trap.

CHAPTER 26

Weaving through Victoria Station packed with home-bound commuters, Martha barely noticed her surroundings. She was so preoccupied with her thoughts she almost missed her stop at West Dulwich. Ignoring the light rain, she trotted home to her team.

Harry opened the door as she walked up the path to her little house. He didn't waste time with conversation, simply turning and heading back to the kitchen, where the other two were waiting along with a lot of freshly brewed tea.

Martha gratefully drank a cup of the reviving brew. Her crew were happy to wait patiently. They knew she would speak when she was ready. She finally put her mug down and recounted the events of the morning. It was a long list but she had a remarkable memory for detail and gave a near verbatim account of what had been said, who had said it, and how long it had all taken. As she was talking, she noticed that Harry had gone quite pink and his eyes were glittering with what she recognised as suppressed anger. He was the first to react when she stopped talking.

As always, he got to the heart of what they were worried about, instantly identifying Tony Green as the man behind all the problems.

"I won't be happy until that man is turned to ashes and scattered off a fishing trawler in the middle of the North Sea — in a force nine gale." Harry was not a man given to bursts of anger. Cool and calculating, that was his normal style, but hearing Martha's account of her morning at the Yard had made him clench his fists.

"Are you sure about the gale bit?" said Julie. "Aren't you worried about blowback? Imagine, being covered by that bastard. Eeuugh." She waved her arms like she was fending off Green's ashes.

The glare she received would have frozen most people, but she just grinned.

"That's better. You don't look so red," she added after a few seconds. "Old geezers like you need to watch their hearts."

"Did you just growl?" Martha asked Harry.

"He does that when he loses his words," said Julie. "Happens a lot nowadays. He does a lot of grunting as well. I think that means he's hungry, or forgotten to eat his bran."

Looking on, Martha thought that Julie was judging her response just right. Harry was at his best when he was calm and collected, not furious as he was at the moment. This intervention would hopefully help to soothe him. Their knockabout sessions could sometimes get boisterous, but they understood where the limits were. It was as though they had some kind of magical road map that allowed them to spot the boundaries. Although heaven forbid that anyone else should attempt the same technique.

Harry made a loud snorting sound, the kind someone makes when they're trying not laugh.

"Not heard that before," said Julie, making an exaggerated show of concern as she added, "Do you think it's some sort of signal old geezers make to attract help from other old geezers?"

She looked slowly around.

"Nope. That's not it. It's just Harry here. The only old geezer in sight."

Harry held up his index finger.

"Ooh look. Hand signals. I can tell this one, it's a rude sign old geezers make when they've been comprehensively done over by the younger generation." She arched her eyebrow. "If I promise not to make you laugh on purpose, shall we get back to work?"

"I think we should," said Martha, wiping away her own tears of laughter. "I'm going to need more tea though. I started this with something important to say, but I can't remember what it was now. You two should have your own podcast. Like my mum used to say, 'You're a tonic.'"

Placing her hands firmly on the kitchen table, Martha looked at her friends. "Let's get started. I want to make sure that we hit that man so hard that he never bothers anybody else again. Who wants to go first?"

CHAPTER 27

It was barely ten miles away but in a city of around nine million it might have been a world apart. Tony Green was back at the mansion and giving his chief operating officer, Mel Taylor, a guided tour. Despite being a man who liked to indulge his murderous impulses, Green could be a remarkably good people manager. In this case, he was careful to give Mel all the time she needed to take in what was on offer and form her own conclusions about how effective the building would be as a new base for his operations. The last thing he wanted was to be surrounded by yes men or women. If there was something wrong with the setup, he was confident that Mel would pick it up straight away and have the courage to tell him.

He needed her second opinion to confirm that he had come across the right place to handle the final disposal of his most valuable assets, where it would happen quickly and efficiently — unless she found some compelling reason not to use it. He understood that his chief operating officer also needed to know she was safe in giving him a negative response and didn't risk being punished for it. It was one of the reasons he made sure that his senior team felt that they functioned like proper business people. Giving his senior

101

people business titles might seem odd to some but to Green it made perfect sense. Mel was the person who made everything work and thoroughly deserved any accolades that came her way. Her skill set was why she was the first person from his team he had wanted to see this place.

Mel was short and muscular with auburn hair and green eyes. He knew from experience that once she was in work mode, her laser focus stopped her from being distracted. Watching her intently, Green suspected she was both pleased and surprised at the location he'd found. Pleased at what it offered and surprised that such a hideaway existed. That's certainly the way he would have reacted. On the way over, he'd given her an overview of what to expect but had been careful to keep the briefing quite general. This really was the case that beauty was to be found in the details. He didn't want her thinking about that until she saw it all for herself.

The property was luxurious, as you would expect in the richest borough of London, with ten bedrooms, all ensuite and a swimming pool with a spa. Green was making sweeping gestures with his arm, like a particularly eager estate agent keen to show off his wares.

Green opened a kitchen cupboard and looked at the contents. "I hope everyone likes baked beans . . . Hopefully it doesn't come to that, even with the quality of our ventilation system, I don't think this place would be very healthy after weeks of all of us existing on a diet of baked beans," he said, on his way into the server room.

Mel followed him inside, brushing past as she took a closer look. She made some notes on her phone, thumbs tapping rapidly. Green was impressed with her typing skills, he was more of a two-fingers man. Seeing her look up, he asked, "Okay?"

"The hardware is all top class so that's good," said Mel. "It passes my test, although I'd like to get an opinion off Gary to be quite certain. He knows how all this stuff works and is a bit of a fan boy when it comes to top of the range gear."

He led them a short distance until they reached a long corridor with doors either side.

"Bedrooms are down there. I'm first on the left but they're all the same." He produced his phone and texted her, making her phone ping.

"Those are the other eight I think we need but feel free to make the case for someone I've missed. I want them in here in forty-eight hours, then we lock down until the job is done. This will be our underground fortress."

"A pretty luxurious one," said Mel.

"That's not all," said Green. "This lovely lady has a few secrets. Follow me."

They walked down the bedroom corridor and turned right, quickly coming to a dead end, where he produced a remote control.

Ten minutes later, a seriously impressed Mel Taylor was back in the kitchen.

"This place is better than I had dared hope. How did you find it?"

"Let's just say the Russians can be easier to work with than people give them credit for."

He produced a cold smile that made Mel suppress a shiver.

CHAPTER 28

Harry was clearly ready to go but waited as Martha reached up to the back of her neck and rubbed at her muscles, which felt hard with tension. She hadn't realised quite how tightly she was wound until Harry and Julie had made her laugh. God, she needed those two. They made grappling with a master criminal, one intent on murderous revenge, seem like a walk in the park. The pair possessed an innate sense of when she needed to be reminded that she wasn't alone and together nothing was impossible. It was as though they knew when she needed help, lifting the weight of responsibility. They always judged it right, not trying to take all the burden from her — that wouldn't work at all. To do her best work, she needed to be close to the centre of events, just not right at the very heart. It was a fine line, a bit of a highwire act, but they usually called it just right.

She pointed at her face and looked at her two friends. "Was it this that gave me away and sent you two off on the comedy routine? How anxious did I look?" she added, answering her own question.

Harry made the faintest of shrugs. He could be remarkably eloquent with his shrugs, using them to convey multiple messages from a "no worries, mate" through to a "you want to take this outside?".

"Your dad used to say the Met was too big for anyone to control it," said Harry. "He used to say that with thousands of officers and civilian staff it was easy for the villains in uniform to get up to all sorts of mischief and everyone was none the wiser. It's why he started tossing back the small fish he caught. He thought dealing with them was time-consuming and expensive and stopped him going after the big guns. It was scumbags like Tony Green who made the money and got their underlings to take all the risks. Not that they needed much encouragement. They might have had a badge but like any common street criminal, they'd nick anything that wasn't nailed down."

Despite herself Martha was always fascinated when Harry came out with these insights into her father. It underlined why he had left her such a complex legacy. On the one hand, he had built a reputation as a scourge of bent coppers, on the other hand, some of his methods could be described as unconventional . . . others were borderline criminal.

Take Harry. Her father had recruited him while he was an active enforcer for a South London crime syndicate. To make it worse, John Munro had paid Harry with money "confiscated" from corrupt officers. It gave Martha a headache just thinking about it and she sometimes wondered why she had joined the police at all. She shook her head. She'd signed up because she loved being a detective and she loved facing the same sorts of challenges her dad had. Catching criminals, whoever they were, was never going to be a simple exercise in "see crook — catch crook". Not in Martha's world.

And she was determined to do it her way.

A polite cough from Harry brought her back to the moment.

"Right, Harry," said Martha. "What would my father have said in this situation?"

Harry produced a shrug. "He'd have said to me, 'Harry. We need to be on our toes for this one.'"

"Stay on our toes," said Martha. "That works for me. Right, Harry, you tell us if you have anything to share. But I've just remembered . . . there's a new problem we're up against."

CHAPTER 29

If the ears of the MI5 woman weren't burning, it would have been a surprise given the way Julie had reacted to Martha describing the way she had been treated.

"It's bad enough that she took a cheap shot at Harry and me. I'm not being funny, but most people at least wait until they've met me before jumping to an opinion." She smashed a meaty right fist into the palm of her left hand, making a loud smacking noise.

Harry reached out and laid his hand on her arm. "I feel the same way but that was some punch. And we want to save those for Green and his nasty little mates."

"Don't worry, there's plenty more where that came from," said Julie, although Martha noted she resisted punching herself again. "It makes me mad the way some of these people put the boot in you, Martha. Do you think they even stop for a minute to remind themselves of what you've gone through? Your mum murdered and little Betty kidnapped . . . and you ending up in prison with a price on your head."

Martha went to make soothing noises but Julie wasn't finished. "That woman had better not turn up in my vicinity or I'll be giving her considerably more than a piece of my mind." Julie lapsed into an angry silence.

Knowing it wouldn't be long before she calmed down again, Harry went to make more tea and Martha went over what she needed to tell her two friends about the morning's events. She'd only been at the Yard for a couple of hours but the time had stretched out to make it feel like she'd been there all day. She wanted to pass on a clean account — one where she told it straight, trusting her formidable memory to recall everything in as much detail as she could. There was too much at stake to indulge in speculation. She had some clear facts to pass.

Her reverie was broken by Harry passing round the tea and some digestive biscuits which, to her dismay, she had accepted and taken a bite from before she could stop herself.

"I know, they're fattening," said Harry as she glared at him. "But everyone knows digestives help with memory and you and I are having a sparring session later today, so you can afford one biscuit."

Martha reluctantly agreed, privately thinking that a session with Harry meant she could eat half a pack and still sweat out the weight gain. She saw Julie take a sip of tea and decided it was time to get back to work.

"As I just told you, this MI5 woman claims to have checked you guys out. She didn't mention you by name but it was obvious it was you she was talking about. In fact, it couldn't be anyone else because you are my only friends.

"What troubles me is that this takes all three of us out of the equation for the task force — which in one way is a blow and in another works for us because it leaves us free to pursue our own inquiries."

She stopped in case either wanted to say something but neither had any questions yet.

"So, the positives I think we can take for now. We know there is actually a task force. It's not much, but at least we know. And every time someone has tried to cut us out, up pops someone with information. Let's keep our fingers crossed.

"I think there were three other important things to come out of today. The Commissioner revealed that the police have checked out reports that Green has changed his appearance possibly with surgery, which we already know. But what was also mentioned was that the informant of this information was no longer available. Which in my world means they have come to a nasty end. I wonder if we can find out who this person was. And when I say we—" she smiled warmly at Harry — "I do of course mean that you should check it out and see what your contacts can come up with. If the Yard has heard a rumour, then I am willing to bet that there's something in it. We already know, thanks to you again, Harry, that he left the country a few months back and your people told you he kept a firm grip on his organisation all that time. We're fully aware that he's back and that I'm on a countdown to a nasty end if we don't get a move on."

"I've set everything in motion," said Harry. "As soon as I hear anything at all, I'll let you know."

"Now I have a couple more things to tell you," Martha continued. "The first one is that I was told that someone, or several people, are actively spreading lies about me. Saying that the only reason I was able to uncover Tony Green was because I was part of his team and turned on him to protect myself."

"What?" said Julie. "Why would they do that?"

"There's no smoke without fire." Harry spoke quietly but his face darkened. For a moment, Martha could see the man who had been a feared gangland enforcer.

"As you say, Harry, someone is trying to muddy the waters and get people to turn against me. Now, I may be reading too much into this, but I suspect that Green is behind these tactics. He's always been all about using distraction to stop people working out what's really going on. It's got all his hallmarks."

"I couldn't agree more," said Harry. "Over the past few months, I've spoken to people who know him and they all say you can never trust any word that comes out of his mouth. The only reason people stay with him is fear. He is utterly ruthless and is said to have people killed just to keep everyone else in line."

"And to think that when I first met him, I thought he was utterly charming," said Martha. "He seemed to genuinely care and wanted to help in any way he could. It makes me shudder to think that was all one big lie." She grimaced. "Anyway, saying Green is a sociopath is telling us what we already know, or suspect. I need to wrap up this morning, so let me finish what I need to tell you. The last nugget concerns Paula Charteris. I was told that she fought my corner, or at least that's how it was presented."

"So, does that make you think you can trust her?" asked Julie. Harry did his Buddha impression.

"About as far as I could throw her," replied Martha.

"Good, that's good," said Julie. "Because Harry and I just can't trust her."

"Well, if we're all agreed, let's come back to this later." She looked at Harry. "Any news on the bugging scheme?"

CHAPTER 30

The best information had come right at the end. Green had been aware there was an attempt to set up a task force and that Paula Charteris was lobbying senior Home Officials to win their backing. Now, it looked as though it was going to happen — or had indeed already happened.

What made the news especially important was the involvement of MI5. His contacts at the intelligence agency were nothing like those he had at Scotland Yard, which probably explained why he hadn't found out about the task force in advance. He breathed a sigh of relief that he had targeted the Commissioner's office. It had taken time and patience for his people to get their feet under the table but this was the first important payback he'd had for his investment. A faint, almost rueful smile played over his face. There were so many times when he had come close to pulling one of his people out — just months before she won a promotion. His pay-off had come today with this news about the task force. And given that the task force would have one target — him — it was vital he had found out.

What he did need to think about was why MI5 was in charge and not the police. A few moments thought and there was no escaping the obvious answer. The old enmity between the police and MI5 had reared its head and this time it was the spooks who had won out. That meant they wouldn't be sharing information with the police quite as freely as he might like. In the past, he had been able to access intelligence information by reading the top-secret updates the agency put out. However, if they were now concerned about security at Scotland Yard, they might keep anything good to themselves. He narrowed his eyes. Everyone was going to have to dial up to maximum effort.

He felt a powerful urge to smoke, even though he had given up at nineteen years old and never touched a cigarette since. He ran his hand through his thick dark hair, much darker than it had been before his face op. He pinched the back of his hand hard, leaving a bright red mark. These were stressful times, so it was hardly surprising he wanted to take his mind off things for a short while, but he had to concentrate on what was before him. As his father was fond of saying, "There's no point wishing you had steak when you're given mince." Pulling his shoulders back in as big a stretch as he could manage, he held the position for a count of thirty, only stopping when his body started producing some popping and grinding sounds. The last thing he needed was to dislocate his shoulder.

Another thought occurred to him. Who exactly was on this task force? He would have to put some very gentle feelers out, see what he could find out. There was one encouraging thing. Judging by the account he had of Martha's meeting with Paula Charteris, it was entirely possible that Martha had been deliberately left off the task force membership. That was very interesting because as far as he knew Martha had the unequivocal backing of the Commissioner, and that should have been enough to get her on the team. If he was right, then it was down to one of two things: Either, for some reason, MI5 felt they were in a position to turn down a direct request from the Commissioner . . . or Paula Charteris was lying through her teeth when she promised Martha she had her back.

Whatever the answer, it felt like he couldn't really lose. What he could do was put more effort behind a couple of campaigns he had been running against Martha. He had always believed that you could cause a lot of trouble by launching a calculated conspiracy theory, one where it was plausible that the target might have done something wrong.

But now you could plant the most unsubstantiated rumours and watch them take off. To his mind, some of the stories were patently untrue. Yet people would willingly join in, seeming to leave all ideas of common sense and trust right behind. It always surprised him the way police officers bit on this sort of thing — you'd think they would know better.

Maybe he should put more effort in and really rock the boat. He rubbed his hands together, pleased at the thought of the misery and confusion he could generate. He went to rub his eyes and, just in time, remembered he had contact lenses in. He was indulging himself again. How many times did he have to tell himself? Sort out the money first, then Martha.

Forcing himself back on track, he put a call into his deputy.

When she answered, he got straight to it. Which was fine by her — she hated wasting time and could think of nothing more irritating than the way some people talked on the telephone, seemingly determined to ask a load of meaningless questions before making their point.

"Boss." It was her usual single word response to one of his calls.

"How's it going?"

"It goes good."

"When?"

"Tomorrow."

He broke the connection and removed the SIM from the burner. That was thrown into the first rubbish bin he came across, the phone having a similar fate a little further on. He sometimes wondered if there was any point in what he was doing but he was a man who believed in better safe than sorry.

As he carried on walking, he brought himself down from what he thought of as a place of cold fury. This was where his anger was so intense he'd had to teach himself how to stop overreacting. In his younger days, his rage ran hot and regularly left a trail of bodies behind him.

This rage was something he indulged, almost looked forward to, because it was so sudden. Many were the times when he had come round to find himself holding a bloodied knife, even a gun, over a body lying by his feet.

But he had to remember that there were two types of criminals — clever ones, who stayed out of prison, and not so clever ones, who didn't. And he desperately didn't want to spend time inside, especially if he was a copper. Even bent coppers had a hard time in the slammer.

He smiled at an old lady who he stepped aside for as they both approached a narrow strip of pavement. In his teens, he would have barged straight through. It wasn't that he'd calmed down or become nicer. He'd have still enjoyed watching her fall. He just didn't need the bother if someone saw him do it.

Green confirmed his decision: money first, then he could relish the time he had with Martha.

It would be a treat. A really big, satisfying treat. But not for Martha.

CHAPTER 31

"We should be tuning in for a breakfast show from tomorrow."

Martha looked steadily at Harry, following his deadpan announcement.

"I take it you're talking about the surveillance kit?" Her heart beat a little harder at the potential development. "You've done well. How did you manage it so quickly?"

"It was a team effort and a few strokes of luck. I can't take all the credit, though, Julie really pulled it out of the bag first thing this morning after you left for the Yard. Perhaps if Julie goes first then I'll pick up."

"I remembered someone I knew from my prison days who told me that they had got a new driving job and she liked to go the gym at seven in the morning so I sent her a nice early message and she got back pronto," said Julie. "As luck would have it she goes to a gym in Peckham so I arranged to meet her nearby and we got it all sorted out over a cup of tea and a bacon sandwich. I told her what we wanted and she was keen to help. In fact, when I say keen, I mean she was as keen as mustard. She got the information we needed in a few hours."

"That was quick." Martha raised an appreciative eyebrow.

"Yeah, well it helped that there are fewer drivers than we expected and she is the kind of woman that slips under the radar. She has got ten possible leads and getting the addresses was dead easy. I passed all the information onto Harry, so I'll let him finish."

"Well, it carried on being our lucky day," said Harry. "My contact, Jenny — and I don't think that's her real name — was able to help. From the ten names, she reduced the list down to four excellent targets. It turns out she knew your dad." Harry checked his watch. "They should have finished the first property by now and I reckon it'll be sorted by late afternoon so we won't actually have to wait until the morning to get the first results." He picked up his mug and took a long swig.

"I'm impressed. I thought it would take a few days at least," said Martha.

"Sometimes the cards fall in the right way," said Harry. "Oh, one thing I forgot to mention. This gear that's being fitted is all the latest stuff, and I mean it was only cleared for use a few weeks ago. The upside, I am told, is that it works brilliantly — the downside is we have to give it back in a week. It's going to be used for bugging the Russian Embassy so we can't be late."

"Bugging the Russians?" Martha's words ended in a squeak. "Have we got our hands on some James Bond type gear? And is that a sensible idea?"

"It is a bit secret squirrel," said Harry. "But for some reason they can't use it until next week. That's why we got our opportunity. And don't worry that anyone will come looking for it. I'm told MI5 people can be a bit anal about sticking to a timetable. That means the first person to come looking for it — officially — is due on Monday afternoon."

"I guess there's no turning back now," said Martha.

"That's the spirit. And Jenny reckons even if they came looking sooner, there's no way it could be linked back to us."

Martha blinked but decided it was too late to worry now. Onwards and upwards. They were committed now.

"Sorry if I came over a bit negative for a moment there. It was when you mentioned bugging the Russians, that did blindside me a bit. But if it's good enough to tackle the FSB, it's certainly good enough for us. And you say this should all be available to us by this afternoon. Very precise."

"It is," said Harry, "and with good reason. Jenny is adamant it should be taken back next Saturday, two days before they will look for it. To help things along she's put six people on it, which will make it very fast." He checked his messages. "Ah . . . I didn't spot this earlier. Two are set up, two to go. They're testing the first two systems now. I'm told it's all voice activated and transmitted directly into the cloud, whatever that means. Apparently, Justin says we can download it straight away and he's as happy as a pig in shit."

"Do you need Justin to explain what you just said there, Harry?" said Julie keeping her face deadpan.

"I shall ignore hecklers."

Justin laughed. "Because this is a luxury system, it has one more thing going for it. It has AI analysis, which allows it to pick up on keywords. It will then instantly transmit that information in digital form to our phones. It's a really brilliant system and saves me wading through tons of transcripts. And we all get to see it at the same time. Best of all, it can identify who is talking so you never get confused by who said what."

"Just when I thought it couldn't get any better — you save the best until the end, thank you," said Martha. "If you don't mind me asking you, Harry, how much is this setup going to cost us? I'm happy to pay whatever it takes but it sounds like this doesn't come cheap."

"You're right about that. This system, with the setup done by her people, and the AI as well, will set you back £10,000 a day."

Martha paled, then rallied. "It will be a bargain."

"You said I was saving the best to last, well, another bit of good news. Jenny told me your dad saved her life. She's letting us have the gear for free."

"I won't pretend that's not welcome news." Relief washed over Martha. "That is all fabulous. Now we just need to find the driver who can tell us where he takes people. I don't know about you guys but I've had quite enough of Green and his sidekicks running around London like they're invisible."

"There is one more thing our modest magician has for you," said Julie.

"Really?" Martha placed her hands on her hips. "Well, don't let me stop you while you're busy pulling rabbits out of hats."

"I'm seeing a contact this afternoon. He tells me he has good information about which horse is going to win the 4.30 p.m. at Epsom later today."

For a moment Martha looked puzzled. "Everyone enjoys a win on the horses, but I'm not sure this is the right . . ." She ground to a halt. "That's a sort of code, isn't it?"

"It certainly is," said Harry. "I've had him out looking for Green."

CHAPTER 32

They'd done it slowly and carefully over the last forty-eight hours but the team were now in place. The eight men and women would be responsible for the final push to make sure the bulk of Green's assets were moved out of the country. Each one had been forced to hand over their phones and sworn to secrecy about where they were working from. With the final pair of the team on site, Green had spoken to them as a group.

"I want you to work fast but carefully. The quicker you get this done, the faster you can leave. I know several of you have to sacrifice family time to do this but it will be worth your while.

"The moment we get wrapped up, all of you will receive a bonus of a million pounds each, paid into an offshore bank account, together with any passcodes you are going to need to access your money."

The eight people looked thrilled. This was big money by any standard.

"Just one more thing," said Green.

All eyes immediately fixed on him and the group went very still.

"You all know I've set aside three weeks for this work and that is what I'm paying the bonus for. But you can double that if you finish in five days or less."

By now, the team were virtually pawing the ground in their eagerness to get started.

"Make it four days and I'll throw in another million pounds each."

This was life-changing money and they burst out in cheers, whistling and stamping their feet.

Green cynically watched on, knowing that none of them would ever receive a penny of the bonus. They would never leave the mansion alive.

He gave them a few seconds. "Let's get going. It's time we made a lot of money together."

They all but ran back to their desks. Green was reminded of the nursery rhyme, 'Three Blind Mice' — with his people as the vermin. The money on offer had blinded them to the reality of their situation . . . There was nothing to be gained by being the richest corpse in the graveyard.

He checked his messages. Ah. There it was, the information he was waiting for. It said that he would be contacted at 2 p.m. Only a few hours to wait.

After sending a brief reply, there was little point hanging around. By this stage, he had nothing to add, it was just down to shifting the right assets to the right locations. After that, another group of people would access it all and move it again. But none of his London team needed to know anything about that.

Grabbing his baseball cap, he made his way back out to the street. He'd given his driver the rest of the day off. He'd either stay on foot or use a black cab. Stepping onto the pavement, he doubted he merited another look with his expensive but dressed-down T-shirt, jeans and trainers. If anyone paid him any attention, they'd assume he was just another wealthy man, possibly a tourist, heading off to buy lunch in the nearby High Street.

Setting himself a brisk pace, he was coming up to the Albert Memorial when his phone rang. As always, the caller was on time. The woman was so obsessed with timekeeping that if she was ever late then he would assume she was dead. He certainly wouldn't take her call because whoever it was, it wouldn't be her.

He answered and she spoke instantly.

"The old shark is smelling blood. The place they met last time. 4 p.m." Message delivered, she even beat him to the punch and ended the connection. She hated being on the phone for any length of time. He'd never known her stay on any longer than she had to and, years ago, had warned him there were too many people listening in.

"Careless talk costs lives," she'd told him. Even back in the day — before we had all this kit, they got that right. It never failed to amuse him that the lessons from the past still held value today.

He grabbed an espresso from a nearby café and checked his watch. The message had told him that the meeting would take place at The Punch Tavern in Fleet Street an hour earlier than given. It was a simple code, probably too simple, but better than nothing. A gentle stroll would see him in the area about half an hour early.

He wasn't much of a drinker, but as he approached The Punch, he was reminded of what a handsome Victorian building it was. According to his father, in the 1970s, the pub had been the unofficial headquarters of many a journalist, especially those from the *Daily Express* and the *Evening Standard*. It had also been a place where journalists and cops could trade information for cash and a few beers. Today, it was a watering hole for tourists and office workers.

Lost in his memories of his father, he almost missed the bald man walking briskly along Fleet Street about a hundred metres ahead of him. Ducking into the closest shop, he felt a thrill of excitement.

Harry was about to take the first part of the bait.

CHAPTER 33

His contact was already standing at the bar. He had a pint of bitter and a shot glass of whisky next to it. As he saw Harry, he picked up the shot glass, drained the contents and slammed it down on the counter.

Harry got the hint. "Two pints of Best, plus give my friend a large measure of your best malt whisky," he told the barman. He rarely drank in the day but the man he was meeting was rarely without a drink and expected you to keep him company.

Del was a stocky six-footer, wearing his usual uniform of an expensive, light grey striped suit with white shirt and no tie. He was bright-eyed and, despite the large alcohol intake, looked hale and hearty.

An ex-copper, Del had served time for taking backhanders from the villains who ran most of the vices in London. From sex to drugs and illegal gambling, if you had the money, they provided whatever was asked for. Del was unlucky enough to have been picked up in a routine anti-corruption sweep but managed to convince investigators he was a small cog in the operation.

In reality, he was an important player and he reported to even bigger players. While he might have been greedy and corrupt, he was far from stupid. His range of contacts included gangland members and both serving and retired police officers. There wasn't much he couldn't find out about.

Throughout the judiciary process, he'd kept quiet about what he knew and made a point of making sure those further up the greasy pole knew he would never rat them out. In return, they were delighted to look after him, with what he needed . . . cash, drugs, women and information among the most useful.

He had been given an eighteen-month sentence, of which he served half in a very comfortable open prison and had emerged back into the world to find he had a lot of people who felt very grateful towards him. Which was just fine by him.

"You're looking well," said Harry. "I see life as a well-paid man of leisure suits you."

"And you look younger than ever, Harry." He took a long pull of his beer. "They do keep their ale in good order," he added.

Nothing more was said for a while. The unwritten rule of these meetings was to never get too personal, and the person who called the meeting set the agenda.

In other words, Harry would have to wait until Del was ready. He hoped it wouldn't be too long — he really wanted to get back to Martha. He was in luck.

"Gotta be quick today, Harry me old mate. I need to get home to see one of my granddaughters who's eighteen today. I've been shopping this morning." He reached down and picked up a Harrods bag with a small, gift-wrapped parcel inside. "Got her a gold chain."

"You've always been generous, Del," said Harry.

"Can't take it with you." Del drained his shot glass and held up his hand to stop Harry buying another. "You know I've always been grateful to you for saving my life that time. Nothing will ever change that. You need a favour, you can always come to me."

Harry looked at his beer for a moment and wondered where this conversation was going.

"Now listen, Harry, and listen well. Tony Green is much worse than you might have heard or imagined. Do you recall Peter Jonson, the dodgy diamond dealer who went missing last year?"

Harry nodded.

"Well, it turns out he tried to double-cross Green. Which was the last thing the idiot ever did. I'm told that Green and his mob took him away and literally sliced him to pieces, starting with his toes, fingers, nose and ears. They sliced his eyelids off so that he had to watch them as they fed the bits to the pigs."

He was warming to his tale but Harry had had enough. "I can guess how this ends."

Del wasn't the least put out. "They took several days over it, I'm told." He turned and made eye contact with Harry. "Trust me when I say the word on the street is he is planning something similar for you guys."

Harry took another swig of the warm ale. "And you don't have any idea where he is, or what he's up to?"

"I've got a little bit more. He has a very tight operation that he was running out of Scotland Yard. It's like the Mafia and run by the code of silence — omertà. No one knows how long he will be around but they say he won't hang about. I've got someone on it but they are having to be super careful.

"The thing about this bloke is he will put business before pleasure, but that just means that when he's finished, he will be able to concentrate all the harder on you guys. Honestly, Harry, the old hands say this is worse than the Kray days."

Harry stared off to the right for a moment. When he looked back, his expression made Del go pale.

"For a minute there, I'd forgotten just how scary you can be, Harry. Please don't think I was suggesting you'd be a pushover. I just wanted to make sure you know exactly what you're up against."

"Not at all," said Harry. "I need to know and thanks for the information. Now, if you don't mind, I need to get going. I have some people to talk to."

Del watched him go. If all the stories were true, perhaps it was this Tony Green who needed to look out.

CHAPTER 34

"Is Harry not back yet? I thought he was doing dinner tonight. I've got all the food he asked for in the fridge."

Julie looked up. "Yeah, he got back about half an hour ago. Muttered something about 'old faces' and then left. He grabbed a bag of stuff and said he'd prepare it round his place. He made a big point of saying he didn't need help so not to follow him."

"I wonder what he's up to," said Martha. "Did he mention anything to you about how the meeting went? He hasn't spoken to me."

"Not a word to me either. He practically ran in here and ran back out again."

"I guess we'll just have to wait . . . At least he's the one cooking dinner, not you or me. It'd be beans on toast or a takeaway if I was in charge. Anyway, since we're spared from food duties, do you fancy a trot to the park with Betty? It's a lovely afternoon."

When they returned, the house was filled with delicious cooking smells that made Martha's mouth water. Harry was stirring something in a pan. Evidently satisfied, he looked up. "Nice timing. It'll be ready in about twenty minutes."

"What are we having, Harry?" Betty jumped into his arms.

"The grown-ups are having vegetable tagine with couscous. You can have the same or egg, chips and beans."

"Can I have the tagine with chips?" said Betty.

"Ooh, and the same for me too, please," said Julie. "Beans would be pretty good as well."

"You may certainly have chips, Betty," said Harry, enjoying watching her smile. He turned an unsmiling face to Julie. "You can certainly not have chips. Neither you or Martha has had a proper meal for a few days now."

Julie thought about making a protest and then saw the determined expression on the old boy's face. *Best not antagonise him*, she thought.

A couple of hours later, the clearing up was done while Martha prepared Betty for bed. She came downstairs to see Harry putting the plates away.

"That meal was delicious. Feel free to make it again," said Martha as she pulled out the kitchen chair. "So are you going to tell us about your meeting?"

Harry avoided eye contact. "Nothing new but there might be a lead to follow up."

Martha wasn't terribly impressed with the response. She had known Harry all her life and knew when he was hiding something.

Putting her hands on her hips, she looked squarely at Harry. "What is going on and who did you meet today? This is not the time to start keeping secrets."

Harry's face fell and he recounted the conversation. Even Julie went pale at the description of the man who had had his eyelids cut off.

"I wasn't keeping secrets, I just thought that it was something that I could protect you from. But I know that was just me being silly and overprotective. What is interesting is that Green is letting it be known in certain quarters that he wants to inflict terrible damage on us all. There's been a total turnaround in his behaviour, says my informant. Green is famous for keeping his cards close to his chest. Apparently, he hates it if people know his business and he never, ever shares information with anyone outside his circle. Now you can't stop him talking about you first followed by us — and he's not playing nice."

Harry took a seat next to Martha. To most people, he would have seemed his usual self, relaxed and happy with the world, but this was a show. He breathed in, then placed his hands carefully on the table before slowing down his breathing. This was one of his favourite calming techniques. In moments, he was composed. "After the meeting with my contact, I spoke to several other people and they have confirmed that Green is liquidating all of his UK assets. They believe he has a deadline of around three to four weeks to get out of the country and disappear for good.

"But the more worrying aspect," he went on, "is that he has crossed some sort of line where there is no off button when it comes to violence and revenge on us. There's a growing belief that he's considering offering a huge reward for our capture. No money has been put up yet but some people are saying if it's big enough, they will be interested. My view is that he will, for now, keep trying to get hold of you himself, using his own people, but at some point soon he will look for outside help."

He looked at Martha and felt a surge of pride at the defiant set of her face. She wasn't going to let Green push her around.

"Okay if I carry on?" he asked.

"Is this something to do with you disappearing for a while this afternoon?" asked Martha.

"It is. I think we need to step up security and assume that he will come after us within a week. We are in a far more dangerous position than I had realised and I don't know if I can be completely confident in keeping you safe."

CHAPTER 35

"Do we think Justin is going to be okay with this kind of maniac?" said Julie. "I don't want to sound mean but I am worried how he would cope in a violent situation where we might not be able to help him."

Harry held his hand up to stop any further conversation. "I think any of us would have a fight on our hands if we met Green face to face. The one thing I do know for certain about Justin is that he has a heart of a lion. He won't take a backward step."

Martha wiped a tear from her eye, hoping nobody would notice. She was glad that Harry of all people had jumped to Justin's defence and she wondered if the wily old fox had worked out what her feelings were for him.

Harry looked at Martha. "We've had a bit of a grim evening but do you two remember a fella called Mad Freddie Fisher?"

"I know the name but he was bit before my time," said Martha.

Julie nodded. "He was a big player back in your day, wasn't he, Harry? In fact, I remember being told that no one came close to you except Mad Freddie Fisher, and that was on his best day."

"You're right. I'm going back forty or fifty years. There were plenty of good operators about back then, but that's not the point," said Harry. "The point is, I learned a lot just from watching Mad Freddie.

"He wasn't the biggest bloke but, like they say, it's not the size of the dog that counts, it's the size of the fight in the dog. His name preceded him. I once saw him go into a pub used by a rival gang. Anyone else would be lucky to get out alive — he brought the place to a standstill. He eyeballed everyone in there, about twenty so-called 'tasty geezers'. Then he just spat on the floor and left. No one dared to follow. They stayed inside in case he was waiting for them. And do you know why he succeeded?"

"I think I can tell where you're going, Harry, but I'd prefer to hear it from the master," said Martha. "We both would," she added, patting Julie on the arm. "When this is over we must have another chat about that book you're going to write."

"Not so sure about writing this down," said Harry. "But back to Mad Freddie and why people were so frightened of him. Everyone in the criminal world knew you couldn't cross him. If you did, the payback was terrible. If he couldn't get you that day, he'd try the next — and keep coming until he'd got his pound of flesh. In every other way, he was a perfectly reasonable man. Show him respect and he'd show it back. He was a real hard man who rarely had to prove it because people knew, absolutely knew, he would find them and hurt them."

"I'm not scared of any man, really," said Martha. "But I might think twice about Mad Freddie. Having said that, didn't I read somewhere that he passed away a few years ago?"

Harry nodded but said nothing.

"Oh, I get it," said Martha. "Someone new has stepped up. So, who is the new Mad Freddie? And do you want to bring them on board?"

"I think it would be a great idea to have them on board — the person I'm thinking about is Lucy Sutton."

"I had a few names in mind but I have to admit I haven't heard of Lucy Sutton," said Martha. "How come she doesn't have a nickname, like 'Lucy the Terrible' or 'Fearsome Lucy'."

"She probably deserves something like that but she doesn't need it. If you know who Lucy Sutton is, then you know you're coming up against the best of the best. Like Mad Freddie, if you start something with her then she always finishes it. She tracked one bloke down to some remote place in Bulgaria and killed him. It took her two years but she found him."

"Not being funny, Harry," said Julie. "But if no one has heard of this Lucy, what's the point of bringing her on to the team?"

"I didn't say no one's heard of her. In the top league of the criminal world, she is widely known and most people will steer well clear. No one in their right mind wants to take her on. She's so determined to have the last word that she's let it be known that if you manage to kill her, she has her own people who will track you down and kill you and your family." He paused to let this information sink in. "I quite like her myself but I'd never want to annoy her."

"When do we get to meet this amazing woman?" asked Martha.

"She's coming at 7 p.m. tomorrow, then she'll let us know the following day," said Harry.

"Let us know?" said Martha. "What do you mean?"

"Julie just asked what the point of this woman is and I think we've covered that, but she will be asking what's the point of us. She's at a stage where she gets to pick and choose her jobs so we need to impress her."

"I'm happy to do whatever you say, Harry," said Martha. "We obviously need this lady."

"She will make a difference, if I'm honest," said Harry. "We're well covered now but I'd be much happier if we could let it be known that Lucy was on the team. When our friend Tony Green issues his reward notice, I'd like as many people as possible to think that even if they got through our defences, they'd never live to enjoy the money."

CHAPTER 36

It was time for Tony Green to throw a bag of spanners in the works. Time to start getting under Martha's skin.

The good news had come this morning when his team announced they were confident they would make the top bonus for moving his assets and, best of all, he no longer needed to be fully hands on. Now he could find the head-space for hitting back.

One thing he knew for sure was that Martha had an Achilles heel in the form of her daughter. In fact, he knew the whole of her motley crew shared this weakness. Tony Green relished the memory of Martha coming close to mental collapse when the little brat was kidnapped. And there was no reason he couldn't make Martha think he might do it again. All he had to do was arrange to snatch a few shots of her daughter and then make sure they reached her. Typical mother, she was obsessed with the girl — Betty, that was her name — so the pictures might unbalance her, make her show her hand.

His second scheme was to cast doubt on her integrity. He'd done a decent job of spreading rumours about her, stories that suggested she wasn't quite the goody two shoes she made out to be. He hoped to build on this work and make it look like she was an active player behind the scenes.

The beauty of his plan was that it didn't matter if it crumbled under the weight of investigation. He only needed a couple of days for it to act as a distraction and persuade a few more people she was dodgy.

The scheme had come to him after he'd learned the identity of the rat who was helping Harry track information about him and where he might be hiding out. His first instinct had been to have him killed. But he'd hesitated. There might be a better plan . . . What if he planted information that Harry would carry back to Martha? That would allow him to act the puppet master and pull the strings.

He'd always believed that the best lies had some truth in them. The idea he came up with utilised that, which meant it carried some risk, but that was okay. Taking risks got you rewards. He turned the plan over in his mind. A few tweaks and he was there. Now he needed to get some information to the rat who was helping Harry.

He dialled a phone number from memory and issued his instructions. "I want it set up today and done tomorrow," he told the person at the other end.

Ten minutes later, Harry's phone pinged with an incoming message. Martha looked up in surprise. Harry didn't often receive messages.

"It's my informant," said Harry. "Says he has something pretty urgent for me. I need to meet him tomorrow."

"Why can't he just tell you?" asked Martha.

"He doesn't like sending information in a text message," said Harry. "He watched something on TV saying how easy it was to grab information out of thin air and has never used it since." He put the phone in his pocket. "Look, it's definitely worth me going. He doesn't make a habit of demanding urgent meetings so I'm prepared to bet he may have something good. I doubt it'll take an hour there and back."

"Whatever you say, Harry. That's good enough for me . . . By the way, we're nearly out of teabags."

"What! I'll buy them now."

Pulling on his jacket, he headed out and politely moved to one side of the pavement as a mum pushing her baby in a buggy walked towards him. He was thinking about his meeting and didn't give it a second thought. She gave him a smile and walked past.

He'd gone a few hundred metres when a new idea broke into his mind. Glancing back, he saw the lady with the baby had disappeared from view — not that it mattered. The pram and the young mother had taken over his thoughts.

What could be more innocent than such a combination? So, did that make the buggy a very good disguise? In this case, not bad — the young mum had walked right past Martha's house. Instead of a baby, the buggy could carry weapons, even explosives.

Standing in the middle of the pavement, he noticed he was at risk of being mown down by a convoy of buggies pushed by parents collecting from the nearby nursery. As he stepped aside, he glanced at the tiny tots strapped into their buggies.

Suddenly, he went cold. How could he even be thinking such things? He doubted he could survive if a youngster died because he'd come up with a bright idea.

He walked on, shaking his head in rebuke, then he stopped again. Just because he wouldn't do it, didn't mean the other team wouldn't. It was something to bear in mind.

CHAPTER 37

As the clock on the oven turned to 7 p.m. there was a sharp rap on the front door.

"I'll get it," said Harry and moved swiftly to let the visitor in.

"If that's Lucy Sutton then I can see why Harry said she's known for never being late," said Martha.

"Maybe she was waiting by the door until it was the exact right time," said Julie.

Further discussion was cut off when Harry walked back in.

"This is Lucy." He waved in the direction of the doorway, where their guest was standing. "This is Martha and the lady with the ever-changing hair colour is Julie."

"A lady, is it now? You must be after something, Harry." Julie stood and offered a hand to Lucy and the two women maintained their grip for a few moments.

"Impressive." Lucy looked at her hand and flexed her fingers.

"You've got a decent grip yourself," replied Julie.

Martha could sense that the big woman was making quite an effort not to let it show how strong Lucy's grip was. It was about to be her turn.

"Hello, Martha. I've heard a lot about you," said Lucy.

They shook hands and Martha waited for the squeeze to come on.

"Don't worry. I only pick on people bigger than me," said Lucy, raising a right eyebrow as she nodded in Julie's direction.

Hand now released, Martha checked out the new arrival. Lucy was about her height and had even broader shoulders. Her chestnut-coloured hair was cut to frame her face — and that's where things got interesting. Martha simply couldn't tell how old she was. The best she could come up with was between twenty-five and forty-five years old.

The obvious thought was that Lucy must have had surgery, but to Martha's eye her skin seemed to be smooth and supple with none of that tautness she associated with facelifts. She couldn't help a quick glance at Lucy's hands. There wasn't much to go on but she did revise her estimate up a bit to thirty to forty years old.

"I'm actually forty-one," said Lucy. "Forty-two next month. It's in the genes. My mum looked about twenty until she was nearly sixty. In my line of work it can be quite helpful to look younger than you are. People tend to underestimate you if they can't judge your age — especially men."

"Well, I hope I look as good as you at forty, but I can assure you that we won't be underestimating you. Not after Harry told us a bit about you yesterday."

Lucy laughed. "Don't tell me. You were expecting some evil-looking woman with gnarled hands and scars all over her face."

"Not quite that bad," said Martha. "But Harry did make it obvious that you weren't a woman to cross. Not that we try to cross anyone. Mind you, Harry did suggest that some people think of you as the new Mad Freddie Fisher."

Lucy laughed to the point of tears. "I've not heard you come out with that one before, Harry, but I will take that as a compliment. I met him once when I was little. He was nice as pie to me and gave me a lemon sherbet." She adopted a more serious tone. "Anyway, all our yesterdays aren't going to get us very far. Harry asked me to come and meet you all and see if we can work together. Now, just to put my cards on the table, I'm already minded to say yes because I know a bit about you."

"Is that a good or bad thing?" said Martha while Julie looked on attentively.

"In both your cases, very much a good thing," said Lucy. "You two first came to my attention when Julie stepped in to stop a nasty little plot to have you, Martha, murdered after your enemies managed to get you banged up in Bronzefield. A very bad place for a copper with no friends."

Martha shivered at the memory. It was one she would never forget.

"You okay to carry on?" Lucy asked, her expression sympathetic.

"Yes, thank you. I'm fine," said Martha. "It's thanks to Julie that I made it out."

"So I was told," said Lucy. "As you know, Harry had put the word out for help and I had a few people on the inside . . . You don't know any of this, Harry, but I was putting together a team of three. I figured that was the minimum, with two more on backup, when Julie acted. She was fast and brutal. A woman after my own heart who scared the crap out of everyone who fancied a pop at Martha." She gave Julie an admiring nod. "Even a hefty reward didn't tempt anyone. It meant my girls could stay in the background and there was never any need for anyone to know about them. Not even you, Harry. Although I promise I would have told you if my lot had stepped in. Within a couple of days, you were out and the immediate danger was over, especially as it meant Harry was now close by."

"And there I was thinking it was only me, Julie and Harry who knew the full story," said Martha.

"I agree," said Harry. "You never cease to amaze me."

"As I said at the start, I like to check people out. I have considered offering you all a job but I decided to stay quiet while you dealt with this madman Tony Green. I knew him through mutual acquaintances and they told me he was a reasonably rational man with a bit too much of a fondness for violence. But Martha appears to have unhinged him.

"There's a story going round that he's recently, as in the last few days, found himself a hideaway in London where he's been behaving oddly. Keeps muttering to himself and walking around looking glassy-eyed.

"I can assure you that comes from someone who would know, which means you all have to swear that you will never repeat that smidgeon of information."

Harry nodded. "I've been told something similar but it's good to get confirmation from other sources."

"Does telling us this mean you are coming on board?" asked Martha.

"It does," said Lucy. "And I'll be in the background. You have solid security already but if things go tits up, I'll be there. You can count on it."

CHAPTER 38

Martha and Julie had turned in early, leaving Harry and Justin downstairs to act as guards and keep each other company. It wasn't strictly necessary, since Harry had four people outside ready for anything, but they enjoyed each other's company and sitting in the peace and quiet. At Harry's age, sleep came less easily. It didn't help that his antennae were flashing 'danger' and he just tossed and turned if he tried to go to bed before 1 a.m. He supposed that drinking gallons of strong tea probably didn't help but he was too ancient to stop now. He decided one more cup then he would head home, leaving security to his team.

The kettle was almost boiling when his phone emitted a soft ping sound. It was just after 1 a.m. Harry rarely got messages and never at this time of night — or morning, if you preferred. He checked his mobile and saw it was Jenny.

Are you awake?

If I wasn't I would be now, Harry replied. *Give me five minutes to get home.*

He headed out of the front door, giving his men a quick thumbs up. Before he left, he had performed a similar exchange with Justin, who had gone upstairs to keep a watch over the two who had gone to bed.

The walk to his house was so short he was home and in his own kitchen in moments. He had to stop himself fidgeting. No one would call at this time of night unless it was important.

His phone ringing shook him out of his thoughts.

"I hope this isn't bad news," said Harry.

"No, nothing to worry about but before I go on, are you sitting on the runway at Heathrow? It sounds like you're next to a jumbo jet just starting to warm up its engines."

"I'm at home," said a puzzled Harry. "It's quiet as the grave here and there's no flights at this time of night." He looked around. "Oh, sorry. It is me. I came in and put the kettle on, just habit really. I need to get a new one, this one makes a right old racket and takes ages to boil. Let me turn it off and then we can talk."

Peace reigned.

"That's much better. Thanks, Harry." He heard her take a breath. "Look, something interesting came up and I knew you'd be awake. I hear you're like me, not one who always gets their eight hours' beauty sleep."

"I'd need more than eight hours," said Harry, laughing. "But you've always scrubbed up well."

"You've got a roguish charm, Harry, never forget that and I reckon I manage on three to four hours sleep a night with a bit of meditation thrown in." She took another breath. "Enough of that. I need to give you a heads up. I've had a couple of people going through the recordings. Three of the drivers were a complete waste of time. They got home, ordered a takeaway and plonked themselves on the sofa for the night with their partners.

"And the conversation — or should I say lack of conversation? Not a word about work. All they did was squabble. About lack of sex, not sharing the housework, always staying in rather than go out. It was so boring, it was a relief when they went to bed and fell asleep.

"But the fourth driver was very different. Turns out he was called in just before he finished for the day and sacked.

140

No pay-off and told if he breathed a word, he would be in a world of bother."

"Did he say why he was sacked?" asked Harry.

"Not exactly but he did say that over the last few days he had been ferrying different sorts of characters to a seriously upmarket house over in West London."

"This is a very interesting piece of information. Is there any way of finding out the exact address?" Harry, who had been pacing around his kitchen listening on loudspeaker, stopped to grab a pen.

"Well, I have a bit more," said Jenny. "Our man is going out at eight tomorrow morning — I should say today, I suppose. He's going to try and sit it out at his doctors to try and get signed off with stress. Says he's going to try for unfair dismissal. He asked his girlfriend to wake him up when she leaves at six."

"Well, good luck with that," said Harry. "Does he know what the people he works for are like? Unless you count a bullet between the eyes as stress relief that may not go well for him."

"What does strike me, Harry, is this might be your best chance to grab him if you are looking for a little chat. He'll be all alone in the house from 6 a.m. and no one expecting to see him until the afternoon at the earliest. I'll send you a WhatsApp with his contact details in a minute."

"Jenny, you're a diamond," said Harry.

"No worries, Harry. It's why I wasn't worried about disturbing you, this is something you needed to know. There is one more thing," said Jenny. "He told his girlfriend that, and I quote, 'Tony Green has lost his head of security.'"

"How could he lose his head of security?"

"Search me," said Jenny. "But this Green doesn't strike me as a careless man. If someone as senior as a head of security has gone missing and the boss doesn't seem too bothered, my guess is he knows exactly what's happened. And I'd bet it involved a bullet in the back of the head."

"That is interesting," said Harry. "As you say, Green is not a man to accidently lose any of his employees, let alone one of his key people, and I agree with you — it must involve Green himself. I think I may have an idea why this has happened."

"Are you going to tell me?" said Jenny. "Or would you have to kill me afterwards?"

"It'll be a cold day in hell before anyone gets through your security, Jenny," said Harry. "This is one of those things that is probably best kept quiet, at least for a little while. If that changes, I will let you know. But, look, when this is all over, how about I take you to a nice restaurant to say thank you. We all owe you for what you've done."

Connection broken, Harry moved into his sitting room to sit in the dark in his favourite armchair. He should grab some rest, even if it was just a catnap. He set an alarm for 4 a.m. and drifted off.

His last thoughts were about Martha and Julie. It was just as well they'd gone for an early night — sleep time was nearly over.

CHAPTER 39

Harry's alarm shredded the dream he'd been having and by the time he was fully awake it was a distant memory. He sat up, stretched his neck muscles and then stood with as little effort as a man half his age. He thought about making tea but it would have to wait — he needed a hot shower.

Half an hour later, the prospect of a busy day ahead put a spring in his step as he left his home. He spotted his neighbour, Danny, a shift worker, heading towards him.

"Morning Mr H," said Danny. "A bit early for you, isn't it? Mind you, if you do have to be up and about, this is the time of year. Nothing better than coming home in the daylight."

Danny was heading for his front door when he stopped. "Can you hang on a moment? I've got an envelope addressed to Martha in my house. I meant to drop it off on my way to work last night but I was in a rush and forgot."

He retrieved it from inside. "Here you go. Hope it's something nice and not a bill." He handed over the envelope and walked back into his house.

Harry managed to keep a look of disgust off his face. He knew exactly who had sent this. What was curious was why it had been delivered to Danny — perhaps the two huge security guards may have been a deterrent.

Harry stood on the pavement looking down at the envelope. Though it was addressed to Martha, there would be no harm in checking the contents.

The pictures of Betty outside her school sent a shiver down Harry's spine.

Stopping outside Martha's house, Harry called to one of the security team. He was pleased to see that it was the team leader, Heather, a blonde woman, who was sitting in the driver's seat.

"We need to step up numbers. From now on, we're going to need two extra people inside the house whenever we're out — and that's starting in an hour from now. From now on, we're on maximum security."

Without wasting any time with questions, she took out her phone and dialled. A brief conversation ensued, then she broke the connection. "They'll be here in half an hour. Is there anything else we need to know?"

Holding the photos, Harry said, "The threat level just went to max."

CHAPTER 40

Harry wanted to be in Brixton no later than 5.15 a.m. He hurried inside Martha's house and called her mobile.

"Harry. What's happening?" Martha always sounded wide awake even if pulled out of a deep sleep.

"I need to brief you and Julie. As soon as you're ready, come down. I'll wake Justin up."

In less than a minute, they were all sitting at the kitchen table in their nightclothes and dressing gowns. Julie and Justin were looking slightly dazed. Martha was staring intently at Harry.

"Sorry to wake you so early but you are going to need to see this." Harry held up the envelope.

No one said anything.

"We may be making some progress. First thing is, we have some results back from your bugging plan, Martha. Most of it was unimportant but we struck gold on one of the drivers."

Julie reached over and patted Martha on the shoulder. "I don't know how you get these ideas but I'm glad you do."

A fleeting smile touched Martha's lips then she looked at Harry. She wanted to hear the rest of the news.

"Turns out one of the drivers was sacked yesterday, without any pay-off and told it was with immediate effect.

By the time he got home — using public transport — he was a deeply unhappy man.

"He talked all the usual bollocks people do in those circumstances, but he did tell his partner one very interesting thing. He said there is a rumour that Green is on the point of making a big move and that he has been ferrying people to some gigantic mansion."

Harry could tell Martha was about to say something so raised an eyebrow at her.

"Do you have an address?" said Martha.

Harry tapped his forehead, looked at Martha, then shrugged and pulled a piece of paper from his pocket. "Just in case," he said. "Julie and I need to be in Brixton by 6 a.m. So you'd better get ready, big girl."

"What's wrong with what I've got on?" said Julie as she headed for the door.

"Before you go, I need to show everyone these."

Harry carefully placed the photos on the table and looked at Martha. "I'm sorry, but you are really not going to like this."

Martha glanced upwards to where her daughter was sleeping peacefully then took another look at the photos before closing her eyes.

"These were wrongly delivered to my neighbour, Danny, who gave them to me a short while ago."

Martha opened her eyes. "You're right, Harry. I'm not happy. And someone will have to pay for this. But right now, the priority is to keep Betty safe and not get distracted."

Justin stood behind Martha, holding her shoulders with a grim look on his face, while Julie studied the pictures, her face going red.

She balled her hands into fists. "Is this meant to be some sort of threat? Over my dead body." Julie looked as terrifying as either Harry or Martha had ever seen her. "There is no way that bastard, or his other bastards, are going to lay a hand on that little girl. I swear that on my own life."

She stared down at the pictures on the table, her knuckles white.

CHAPTER 41

"How do we handle this, Harry?"

He sat back in his chair and folded his arms. "There's no way we can send her off again. She's like you, Martha, so we have to believe her when she says she will run away. And let's face it, there isn't any of us who hasn't been worn down by her relentless ringing. She's a clever little so-and-so. She's pushed us into allowing her to come home in the first instance, so sending her away again is never going to work, and again just like her mum would do, she will find her way home. Realistically, she's not giving us a choice. But it is your call."

Martha had been listening intently. "She sobbed in my arms a few nights ago and said being away had given her nightmares about me dying. I calmed her down and I don't want her to go through a separation again — hell, I don't even want to go through it myself. But . . ." she said, her jaw jutting in determination, "I have said I'll take her there myself if it keeps her safe. Though actually, I've concluded she will be better off at home. I just hope her nightmares ease off. I mean, it's great to have her back to talk to and cuddle, but at two fifteen in the morning? I have enough sleeping trouble as it is."

"I'm with you," said Julie, dabbing her eyes with some damp tissue paper.

"Did I mention that I hate Tony Green?" Martha handed a fresh tissue to her friend. She looked at Harry, who was taking a sip of his tea. "You just said you had concluded that Betty was best off here. Do you want to explain why?"

"Well, as we just discussed, short of clapping her in irons we'll never keep her away, and the thought of her wandering around the countryside in the middle of the night is too awful for words. I'm certain that this is now the safest place for her. Since the last time we've improved security here no end. And with immediate effect, I am tightening it even more, doubling up on the people here. Plus, whenever we go out, I will have someone inside to ensure no one tries to sneak in by coming through the neighbour's loft, or getting into the back garden.

"And if that wasn't enough, we have Lucy on board, and her team will be armed to the teeth. She's up to date with what's happened and she will be over later on.

"Right, Julie, unless you want to be arrested when we get to Brixton, get out of those strawberry PJs and put something sensible on."

Julie gave him the bird as she headed for the door.

CHAPTER 42

"I've just got to pick up some cash, you get the car started."

Before she could reply, he was gone.

Minutes later, he was dumping the sports bags on the back seats. He nodded to them. "I just thought it might be easier to get some sense out of our bloke if we go good cop, bad cop. You slap him around a bit, then I produce the cash and tell him, instead of a kicking, he can have a barrowload of money. I know which way I'd go."

"Spoil sport, you're just out to stop me slapping him into next week."

"Well, it did occur to me that it might be easier to understand him if you don't finish the job of loosening all his teeth."

"Do you always keep so much money under your bed?"

"Saving for a rainy day, you might say, and this might be just the day," said Harry.

"If you're looking for anyone else to hand over some cash to, don't forget me." She thought for a moment then added, "I was sort of joking about that."

"No you weren't."

"You're right. I wasn't joking. Shower me with notes whenever you like."

"Right, let's go. That's enough fun for today," said Harry. "When we get there, we drive past and then park a few streets away. If anyone else is lurking, we need to get rid of them, pronto."

"Do you really think someone might be there?"

"We're dealing with Tony Green," said Harry. "Rule number three says that whenever you tackle a nasty little bastard, be very careful."

They set off in silence, the five-year-old Audi saloon gliding along smoothly.

"The place we want is up towards Brixton market. It's a small ground-floor flat," said Harry.

Julie drove in that direction, careful not to draw attention by going too slowly or quickly. They passed a little Victorian terrace and Harry declared he couldn't see anyone else loitering around.

"Hang on." Julie glanced in her rearview mirror. "Don't turn around, but a woman has just come out of there."

"Would you say she's about mid-twenties with brown hair?" said Harry.

"I think so," said Julie. "I only saw her in the mirror but I got a clear enough look."

"Great," said Harry. "Now, can you park here or is it residents only?"

"Residents only, I'm afraid. I spotted a place a short walk away when we drove down here so I was going to leave it there."

"In that case, let me out here," said Harry. "I'll scout around on foot while you park."

He reached behind him and grabbed the sports bags and a small, brown Amazon box. "I'm hoping this will get him to open the door."

"I like your thinking, Harry. Shall I see you here? I won't be long."

He flashed her a thumbs up as he jumped out of the car. Looking around, he decided to walk back to the flat where the bugged driver, Tom Rykes, lived. He crossed the road and doubled back to where Julie had let him out of the car. He wasn't worried if hidden watchers spotted him. If they did, they would have to show themselves and then he could deal with them.

He passed the front door of the flat and still no one could be seen. Good, they were alone.

As he waited for Julie, he noted the commute to work had already started. Time was ticking and he needed to get inside that flat soon. They would make their move at 6.30 a.m. Rykes was probably used to being up and about early so it would be a good time to knock on his door.

Decision made, he leaned against a lamppost and hoped that Rykes would be sensible. One way, he was left with a lot of money, the other way — well, the other way was not a good place to find yourself. Not that he was overly worried about Rykes. It was Julie he was thinking of. If Rykes made a bad call, she was likely to do some seriously unpleasant things to him, and Harry didn't want her to be put in the situation where she could find herself facing serious charges. Even the prospect of murder could not be ruled out. She was very big and carrying a great deal of rage that could easily unload on Rykes. If that happened, he suspected the police would put two and two together, come up with whatever figure they liked and charge him too.

And that would mean trying to convince a jury they were both innocent of all charges. There would be no chance of that. She had as many tats as he had old charge sheets. They'd be banged up by the end of the day.

There would be no chance of calming her down. But what could he do? Julie knew all about his past so if he tried to rein her in, she'd laugh at him. Accuse him of "grandadsplaining".

No — the best hope was that Rykes took the cash and talked his head off.

Someone tapped him on the shoulder. His heart in his mouth, he spun round and saw Julie grinning at him.

"Nice spin for a pensioner," she laughed.

He scowled and then grinned. "I know I've said this before but you aren't half light on your feet for such a big bird."

She smirked, irritatingly. "So, what's the plan?"

"Simple, I hope," said Harry. "We walk back up there and knock on the door. Now, listen carefully: This is the only part that requires a bit of thought. When I knock, I'll be standing on his doorstep. He'll be looking at me and looking at the package. I will step back and to the left — his right — and all the time I'll be saying it's a special delivery and my bosses have given strict instructions that I deliver directly to him, not leave it outside.

"The next bit is down to you. You will be standing on the right, his left. You're against the wall, out of his eyeline. And in any event, for just a moment, he will be wondering what's in the parcel and not worrying if there might be someone in his blind spot. The moment I stop moving, you step out, grab him and lift him back into the house. At this point, he may want to start shouting but because you have stuffed his mouth with this—" he produced a cotton handkerchief — "he won't be able to make a sound.

"I will follow you inside and close the front door. You then get me to hold him while you zip-tie his hands, then we explain things to him."

"You're a dark horse, Harry," said Julie. "You're using a bit of psychology there, aren't you? It's not true that you're just a 'kick 'em in the balls' kind of guy. Let's get going."

They walked briskly and took up their positions at the front door.

"Harry?" said Julie. "What happens if this doesn't work?"

"Then we follow Rule Two."

"Rule Two? You've definitely never told me what Rule Two is."

Harry ignored her expression and knocked sharply on the front door. A few seconds later, he did it again, then again. After the fourth knock, he heard a muffled shout. He knocked again. Now the voice was louder.

"It's six thirty. Who's out there?"

"Amazon delivery, sir. Sorry to wake you but I've been told that I must give this parcel directly to Tom Rykes."

"What's in it?"

"I just deliver sir, sorry."

"Okay, give me a second."

The door opened and Rykes's eyes went to the parcel Harry was holding out in front of him.

Harry stepped back, to his left, and Rykes couldn't help but lean out of the door. It was as though the parcel had a special magnetic effect that worked on him alone.

Harry took one more short step then stopped.

Cue Julie.

CHAPTER 43

For such a big woman she was, as Harry had just noted, remarkably light on her feet. She didn't so much walk as glide smoothly over the surface. She was also deceptively fast and she hadn't hesitated when Harry sent the signal.

She appeared in the doorway, grabbed Rykes firmly at the top of his arms and lifted him back inside. Harry was right behind her, pulling the door closed behind the second they were in.

Rykes was bewildered. One moment, he'd been staring at the parcel, hoping it held something valuable. He'd even started to dream that maybe it was a pay-off from Green. The next moment, a giant woman had picked him up like he was made of cotton wool.

To his surprise, the woman, still holding him off the ground, turned in the tight space of the entrance to face the old boy who had been holding the parcel.

His bewilderment switched to fear and he made to start shouting for help. But before he could even finish taking a breath, the woman shoved something in his mouth, forcing it right in until it scraped the back of his throat and he couldn't make a sound, let alone yell for assistance.

He didn't notice but Harry and Julie exchanged a look that said, *That went pretty well.* Harry checked the hallway, ignoring the bikes leaning against the wall and noted a door was open on the left as he looked down, and on the right was a staircase leading to what he assumed was the upstairs flat.

He shook Rykes hard. "Does that open door lead into your flat?"

Rykes tried to speak but only managed a vague squeaking sound.

"Just nod your head for yes, shake it for no, said Harry."

Rykes panicked and at first shook, then quickly changed to a nod.

"Don't piss about," said Harry. "Which is it, yes or no?"

This time Rykes nodded vigorously.

"All right, all right. I get it," said Harry. "We're going in there now. I take it you're home alone?"

This was greeted with more nodding.

Julie carried in the whimpering Rykes and Harry followed with the two bags. They looked around and saw there was small settee in front of the television, a galley kitchen and a folding table.

"Grab that chair by the table and put it in front of the settee," said Julie. "I'll plonk him on the chair and you cuff him."

Harry lifted the chair over and a few seconds later, Rykes was zip-tied and going nowhere.

"I imagine you are wondering what we want from you." Harry managed to induce menace into a simple question.

Rykes nodded furiously.

"Okay. Now I'm going to trust you here. I'm prepared to take the hankie out of your mouth," said Harry, "but if we do that, you are going to have to swear that you won't start shouting. Because if you do, we will punish you. Do you understand?"

More nodding.

Harry looked at Rykes for several seconds then nodded at Julie, who had moved round to his side. At the signal, her hand shot out and yanked the handkerchief out of his mouth.

Rykes looked startled then started moaning. Harry held his finger to his lips. "No noises, please. But you can have a drink."

Julie was already pouring water into a glass and held it against the man's mouth.

"Not too much at first," she said. "Nice and slowly."

Rykes sipped the water until he'd had half the glass and Julie took it away again.

"That's enough for now," she said.

Rykes went to ask for more but Harry tapped him on the knee.

"Look at me, please. As you can see, we are prepared to be reasonable. So, let me join the dots for you. We could obviously have easily killed you by now, and your girlfriend for that matter. We watched her set off this morning.

"But we haven't done that, so, if you think it through, it's because you are more useful alive and that means you have something we are interested in. Just to help you — we're not after a physical item, which means you must know something. We want you to tell us what we need to know."

Julie stepped in with more water and this time he drank carefully as he drained what was left. He went to speak but Harry silenced him with a raised hand. "Let me finish and then you can speak."

Rykes nodded.

Harry reached down to the side of the settee and picked up the sports bags. He unzipped one of them and showed the inside to Rykes, who went bright red.

"Well done," said Harry. "I think you're beginning to piece it together yourself. There's two hundred and fifty grand in there and the same in the other one. Tell us what we need to know and it's all yours. Plenty of money to start again, maybe a little beach bar in South America. I don't mind where you go, just so long as you're gone tonight and don't leave any trace. That includes the girlfriend. If she's not coming with you, then you mustn't tell her anything.

"Now, before you think this is too easy, there are some rules. The biggest one is don't lie to us. We know enough to tell if you do."

He looked at Julie and then back at Rykes.

"Let me tell you about my associate here. If you make her angry, you will, in the last moments of your life, wish you hadn't."

Julie put on one of her scary faces, a sort of blank expression supported by a thousand-yard stare. She always claimed she had picked it up from Harry. Whatever the truth, it always worked, especially as she managed to inject a strong note of barely suppressed rage.

It certainly had an effect on Rykes, who went very still, looking anxiously at Harry to see if he could find any empathy there.

No chance.

"So, which is it?" said Harry. "Painless and rich — or lots of pain then death?"

"Th-the first one. Please don't hurt me."

CHAPTER 44

Martha waggled her phone at Lucy.

"Before we go any further, I need to call Justin. He's been absolutely brilliant looking after Betty and needs to know what's going on. You need to meet him anyway, because he's always around."

"That sounds like a good plan," said Lucy. "Before you ring, tell me a bit more about him."

"All right, why not?" said Martha. "We were together for a few years. Had Betty quite quickly and although we both loved each other to bits, still do, we were too young, got on each other's nerves. We separated for a while, but recently we've got close again and I will admit that once this is over, we are looking to get back together again."

"That's lovely. I hope it works out," said Lucy. "Please forgive me prying but it helps me to know how strong your relationship is as things are going to get quite meaty. Now, what about your man's fighting skills? He couldn't have much better teachers than you, Harry and Julie."

"He's as brave as a lion and as much use as a fried egg," said Martha, who had clearly struggled to find the right words.

"I see. That actually makes things easier. If anything happens, he just needs to grab Betty, get as low as possible and wait for it to end," said Lucy. "We could keep the egg theme going by giving him a frying pan. One of those old-school French ones can be lethal and you don't need to be very accurate with your hitting."

"No frying pan, I think," said Martha. "He'd be more likely to hit himself. Anyway, we're a very modern couple. If there's any punching to do, that's my job."

"Yes, I've been told that Harry has done a great job with you. Some say you could be a pro fighter with a jab that rattles your fillings."

"Yes, he's a brilliant teacher and I was a very willing student. He started teaching me when I was younger than Betty is now. I really enjoyed it."

"Ever thought about teaching Betty?"

"I have," said Martha. "But I want her to ask rather than be pushed. She's like my mum, her grandma. Smart as a whip but a very gentle woman." She stopped and smiled at Lucy. "I barely know you, yet I've been franker with you than I would normally be with someone."

"Well, thank you for that." Lucy sketched a bow. "Now, Julie, the final member of the gang. Anything I need to know about her?"

"Don't annoy her," said Martha.

"I must admit that I had heard similar, including from one would-be Jack the Lad who experienced sudden teeth loss," said Lucy. "He became very emotional when I asked him who did it. Not that he didn't deserve it." She glanced at the time showing on the oven. "Is that clock accurate?"

"I think so," said Martha.

"As you may have noticed, I'm a bit of a freak for punctuality," said Lucy. "Now, we need to discuss how we're going to do this. My two men should have shown up by now. They'll be waiting outside, but I don't want to bring them in until you and I have found a place for them."

She glanced around the cosy but small kitchen then walked up the hallway to the front door and went outside. Martha poured herself a glass of water and sat at the round kitchen table.

It was just after 6.45 a.m. and she felt like she'd already done a full day's work. Betty would be up in a short while and she wanted things to, at least on the surface, appear nice and normal. That definitely meant ensuring there were no people with guns wandering around.

Thinking of Betty reminded her that she had meant to ring Justin. He had gone back to his flat to have a shower and grab more clean clothes. She was about to call when she stopped. He was going to be walking Betty to school. He was probably already on his way. She might as well wait for him to get here.

She wondered how Harry and Julie were getting on.

CHAPTER 45

Tom Rykes was rubbing his wrists. Julie hadn't been gentle when she tightened the zip ties and he was red raw where they had dug in. He'd tried flexing but they were too sore so now he was reduced to blowing on them.

"You should probably get some cream on those," said Harry. "Got anything like that? We're fresh out."

"There's a bit of stuff in the bathroom," said Rykes. He started to lever himself up.

"Hold on a minute there." Harry pressed him back down in his seat. "Just tell us where to look and my associate will get it."

"Go through the bedroom—" Rykes pointed at a door that was slightly ajar — "into the ensuite and you'll see a small white cabinet. There should be something in there."

Julie came back with a tub of cream and a bottle of antiseptic. She waved them at Rykes, who paled. "Not that antiseptic, that'll sting like mad. Just the cream, please."

Gingerly he applied some ointment, huffing and puffing as he went. Julie rolled her eyes at Harry. "Can we get on with it?"

"Yeah, sorry," said Rykes." Just give me a sec, this is making it feel better."

A few more dabs and he was ready.

"How long have you worked, or did work, for Tony Green?"

Many years ago, Harry had learned to start with the easy stuff.

"I was with him for nearly fifteen years and never let him down, even if I say so myself. But yesterday I got a call from Jack Thompson — one of Green's gofers — telling me I was out. Not a word of thanks or any money."

"And this Jack Thompson, did he operate out of an office?"

"I don't know about any office, all my instructions usually came through encrypted messaging. All I did was turn up at the garage and pick up the car that was allocated to me. I only rang if there was a problem with the car, which only happened once when I got a puncture."

Harry nodded as if he was taking all this in but in reality he was broadly aware of the way Green operated. What he needed were details, and he was about to find out if Rykes was any use.

"Tough way to lose your job," said Harry. "Were you given any information that might explain why they threw you under the bus?"

"Not from Thompson," said Rykes. "When I tried to ask him, he just told me to 'get on with it' and broke the connection." He stopped talking, his chest visibly falling and rising as if he was short of breath.

"I need everything you've got. I do mean everything," said Harry. "If you need to compose yourself then do so. But when you do start talking, I expect to hear things I don't already know."

"Understood. I'm ready," said Rykes. "A bit of background. There's a little group of us, three in fact, who talk to one another from time to time. We all work in different areas. There's me, Diane on back-office stuff and Geoff in security.

"Green may pay well but it's no walk in the park. People disappear for no reason so we try to cover for one another, you know, sort of act as an early warning system. We've never had to activate it, so far, but being warned in time could save our lives. Give us a bit of a head start."

"How come the three of you are working together?" said Harry. "I heard that Green likes to encourage his staff to stab one another in the back . . . he doesn't like people getting to know one another, or make friends."

"It's a good question. We all started at the same time, more or less, which means we have a lot of shared history and information about ourselves, which if passed to Green would be very bad news. You can be sure that if one of us turned on the others, the response would be nuclear."

For a moment, Rykes looked as though he was unsure of what to say next but the moment passed. He rubbed his eyes and was about to carry on when Harry interrupted, "You shouldn't rub so hard. You can damage your eyes."

Julie stared at him, clearly wondering why he'd made the statement. Harry shrugged — it was a pet hate, although perhaps here wasn't the moment. He waved Rykes on.

"Okay, so bear with me now because this is the heart of it. A couple of weeks ago, Geoff got sent to Heathrow Airport. He was ordered to drop everything and head there straight there. He was told to spend a couple of hours in the arrivals and to see if he could spot any MI5 people — and I quote — 'lurking about'. It was all a bit ridiculous really but he stuck at it for a couple of hours then rang his boss to say he'd seen nothing.

"He thought that would be it but they told him to leave the airport and sent him to Eaton Terrace. He was told to walk around and not be conspicuous. Then his orders were, 'Go home and forget this day ever happened.'"

"He did as he was instructed. And he did try to keep it secret but, in the end, curiosity got the better of him. When he finally told us, we couldn't make sense of it either, until Diane heard something a few days later."

Rykes licked his lips and nervously rubbed his hands on his pyjama trousers.

"Could I have some more water?" he said. "I'm feeling a bit dry."

Julie handed him a full glass. She doubted he would choke now the initial shock had worn off.

He downed the drink. "Thanks. Now, as I was saying, Diane picked up a rumour from one of the senior people. He said the boss had flown back into London a couple of weeks before this strange event and had spent his first night at some expensive place close to Sloane Square.

"The three of us talked again and agreed it was likely Geoff had been sent to check it was safe for Green to fly back. And that's the first time in months that he's been heard of in the UK. But that's not all that's happened. Diane was told to finish what she was doing and go. No warning, but at least they gave her some money, unlike me.

"Ever since then I've been waiting to get let go as well, but I never thought they wouldn't pay me something . . . bastards. Anyway, that's it. We all agree that Green will be leaving the country very soon and, by the looks of it, not coming back."

He finished and looked at Harry and Julie. But as the silence grew, he became more uncomfortable, especially with Harry's deepening frown.

"Bollocks," said Harry, making Rykes jump.

"What do you mean? I've told you what I know — why the threatening expression?" said a trembling Rykes.

"I asked for everything. You're holding something back — I can read you like a book. So, you've got five seconds or we get to work on you."

"No, I've told you it all," Rykes squeaked.

"Four."

"Three."

Julie stood up and flexed her hands.

"Two."

Rykes cracked. "He's had a facelift — doesn't look like himself anymore."

"I don't know how to break this to you, sunshine, but we know all about that," said Julie.

164

Rykes looked miserable. "There's no more, I promise."

Harry had already decided that was the case. In fact, he was pleased that such a small cog had been able to supply such solid information. Admittedly, it wasn't totally new news, but it did help shore up what they already knew.

"There's one last thing that is puzzling both of us. Where exactly on Eaton Terrace? Was your mate Geoff given a number?"

Rykes looked miserable. "He was only told to walk around Eaton Terrace, nothing more. And as anyone who has worked for Green will tell you, he's a man who likes his mysteries."

"Sorry, can you expand on that?" said Harry.

"He made a habit of never being dropped at his intended destination. You could never tell where he was really heading and wouldn't want to get caught following him. He is a nasty bastard."

Harry looked over at Julie, who nodded.

"Excellent," said Harry. "And that barely hurt at all, did it? We're going to leave you now, with your money. I suggest you get moving. Don't take this personally but I don't entirely trust you. I bet that even now you're wondering if you can turn this to your advantage. Well, I'd forget that idea. You see, we're going to give you a couple of hours' head start then we'll let your organisation know you've been talking to us. They'll be round here like a shot, eager to speak with you."

"You wouldn't." Rykes had gone grey.

"I wouldn't recommend you staying around here," said Harry. "Oh, just to make it interesting, we'll let them know about your little Gang of Three."

"You bastard, you absolute bastard." Two spots of bright red formed on his cheek bones.

Julie patted him, none too gently, on the face. "You didn't think we would let you go just like that? Never mind, soonest mended and all that, but don't waste time saying naughty words, you gotta get a move on. I'll keep an eye on the news, to see if any headless bodies have been found with a bag of loot."

Harry and Julie set off for the car.

"You know what, old man?" she asked Harry. "I probably enjoyed that last little bit rather more than I should have. He was a nasty little shit working for an even nastier bunch of shits. Did you really give him half a million quid?"

Harry chuckled. "Don't be daft, it was nowhere near it. I think there was about a grand in the first bag and my dirty gym gear in the second. As you say, he was a nasty little shit working for an equally nasty bunch of people."

CHAPTER 46

The two women were sharing a fresh round of tea in the kitchen as they grabbed what would be just a few minutes of freedom before Betty woke up and the outside world poured in. While she had been told Martha was formidable, seeing her close up was enlightening. She could tell that Martha was a woman who took responsibility of caring for her team very seriously. Lucy was paying close attention as Martha set out some ground rules. They were non-negotiable.

"I know we can't anticipate every single thing," she said. "If it gets to the point that we are going to be overrun, then we stop. I'm not willing to see anyone die in my name, especially not Harry, Julie or Justin. And I say that because I know they want to protect me. And I would say that to their faces."

"I can see that," said Lucy. "You're a passionate woman, which I really like about you." She drank her tea and waved the mug at Martha. "Always take tea when you get the chance. I'm like Harry in that way. But back to where we were. I can't control every single moving part in this — any more than you can, any more than Tony Green can. What I aim for is a layered defence with you, and those most precious to you, at the centre.

"At each layer we take out the enemy by focusing on stopping as many as we can. But the point is not to worry about stopping everyone, because any mercenary who gets through will be picked up by the next layer, and so on. If anyone makes it through the final layer, they are going to find themselves very short of friends and facing our guys."

Martha was impressed with this woman's easy self-confidence, but she still had questions and every intention of asking them.

"I accept what you are saying," she said. "But I'm in charge of everything that's happening here, so despite your analysis, I do have some questions. I warn you in advance, nothing personal, but I am very direct as you have most probably noticed."

"Fire away." Lucy chuckled. "And I have heard about your reputation for taking no prisoners, which is why I wore my big girl pants today. I shan't take offence."

"Thank you," said Martha. "I think I understand your layered defence strategy and I'm sure we'll have a more detailed discussion about it. But I'd like Harry and Julie to be involved in that. For now, how many layers of protection are we going to need?"

Before she could answer, there was the sound of tiny feet charging down the stairs and then Betty appeared, giving her mum an indignant stare. "I don't mind you having friends around, but you promised me breakfast in bed. Now it's too late."

CHAPTER 47

"Toast?" Martha looked around the kitchen and could see nothing that resembled an easy-to-put-together meal. Her hand hovered over a single grapefruit in the fruit bowl, which she picked up and showed to Betty.

Her lip curled in disgust. "I was promised homemade blueberry pancakes with maple syrup."

Martha, who had just been lauded for her qualities of leadership and staying cool under fire, experienced a mounting sense of panic as she faced her determined five-year-old. She was going to have to throw herself at her daughter's mercy.

But she was spared further humiliation when Justin walked in holding a carrier bag, which he held up to head height.

"Blueberry pancakes, wasn't it?" he said, quickly putting the bag down as Betty charged across the kitchen for a hug. He spent the next half an hour cooking pancakes for Betty. Then, before he could wash up, Harry and Julie arrived.

Julie's eyes lit up. "Pancakes. Lovely," she said. How many can I have?"

Justin rolled his eyes but quickly mixed up a fresh batter.

Julie watched him working. "It's a good job you and the old geezer can cook . . . gives us ladies a chance to think big thoughts."

"The last time you had a big thought you had to lie down," said Harry, making a dismissive "pah" sound.

Before Julie could respond, Lucy walked into the warm kitchen, having been outside organising her security team. Both Julie and Harry instantly switched from light-hearted bantering to full-throttle focus.

"Hello, Harry, good to see you and Julie are back. Perhaps we can catch up later?" said Lucy. "In the meantime, I wouldn't mind your advice. As part of the general tightening of security I'd like to station a couple of people in the house . . . What do you think? Is the house big enough?"

"I had same thought but we will need to get Martha to make the final decision on that," said Harry.

"Okay, that's fine but I'm trying to get everything pinned down so I can have my best people in the best place. In other words, right here." Lucy emphasised her point by jabbing the table with her finger.

Harry shook his head. "I get what you're saying but Martha makes the decisions. No ifs, no buts. Not in a bad way, she's no tyrant but sets the tone. Martha is the boss. Full stop."

Martha's appearance downstairs was heralded by the sound of thundering feet as Betty charged ahead of her. She burst into the kitchen and instantly spotted Justin was still clearing up. "Come on, Daddy, you know it's art class today."

"Don't worry, I got everything ready last night," he said. "Wouldn't want you being late for your favourite."

Martha looked surprised.

"She's showing a talent for using colour, so I'm told by the school. They want to encourage her for a while, see where it goes," explained Justin.

Martha felt a tightening in her chest . . . How had she missed this key moment in her daughter's life? She should be sharing the experience with her, helping her develop if she did have a talent.

Justin could tell by her expression that she was upset at missing out. "I did tell you," he said. "But you've had a lot on your plate. You can't do it all. Look, if it works out, she will be doing it for years. It could be just one of those phases and next month it will be football."

She wasn't really consoled by this but hid it from Betty as she gave her a hug. After her daughter left, she thumped around the kitchen before taking a deep breath. "I need to concentrate or I'll end up doing nothing at all. I almost had a go at Justin, but it was my idea that he concentrated on our daughter."

As Harry watched her, he marvelled, not for the first time, about how quickly Martha could regain control. Rather quicker than he could, he thought as she looked at him patiently. "I said, how did you two get along this morning?"

His phone announced an incoming message. It was such an unusual event that both women stared at him. He was going to leave it but suddenly got a powerful urge to see who was trying to contact him.

As he checked the name, a shiver of apprehension ran down his spine. It was his contact. The last time they had met they had agreed that they would only make contact if it was urgent.

He read the message.

See you at noon. Ted.

Ted was code for "urgent" and you needed to take two hours off the time stated. He'd better get going.

"That was my contact," he told Martha. "I need to see him — now. Julie can fill you in about this morning."

He set off for Victoria Station.

CHAPTER 48

Harry walked through the ticket barrier at Victoria Station. He noticed Del straight away sitting at a table outside a café reading a paper.

Before he could get close enough, Del stood up and headed out of the station. Harry could do nothing other than follow him and wonder what it was that had so clearly spooked the guy. They carried on towards Victoria Coach Station then crossed the road into a side street with a small Victorian pub that had somehow resisted the tidal wave of development in the area. Inside, Del ordered two halves of bitter then took the glasses to a table at the back.

"Sorry about the drama but the CCTV in this place only works at the bar. I know the owner — he runs a place where people can relax without worrying about being recorded. I needed to get out of Victoria, that place is alive with cameras. The only saving grace is there's so much footage it's difficult to get through it."

He took a long pull of his beer, almost draining his glass. Harry was surprised at the general lack of customers. It was just them and the landlord, a taciturn man with a pallor as grey as his hair. He was drying glasses with a tea towel.

"I know it's a bit early but why are we so alone?"

"It can take a very, very long time to get served if the landlord doesn't know you," said Del. "The man here is ex-Special Branch. Those blokes know how to keep a secret. And they're very good at attaching names to faces."

As they spoke, a couple of office workers came in. The landlord turned on his heel and walked swiftly through a door and disappeared from view. The couple stared at each other before the woman said, "If he doesn't want our money, I don't see why we should hang around."

They left after casting curious looks at Del and Harry and could be heard complaining about "pensioners with all the time in the world getting a drink."

"Can I get you a refill?" Harry asked Del, who held his nearly empty glass up to the light, then, with a sigh, put it back on the table.

"I've got a long day ahead, Harry, so I will regretfully have to pass on your offer." He sat lost in thought. After a couple of minutes, Harry was beginning to doubt he was right about how urgent things were. So far, they had gone for a walk, ordered beer and found a bar that looked like it could be run by the Freemasons.

He couldn't spend too much time on this — there was a lot to do. Even getting Betty to school every day was proving to be a challenge. He needed to make sure that situation was back under control.

"Sorry to push you, Del," said Harry, "but life's a bit hairy at the moment. And you just said you are busy as well. Would it be better if we rearranged this meeting?"

Del tugged at his baseball cap, seeming to try and adjust the fit without making any particular progress.

"Sorry, Harry. After I messaged you, I got another call that has made things more complicated."

"Not sure I understand." With anyone else, he would have been exasperated, but he and Del went back a long way. "This new information you've got, are you now worried that what you knew before is wrong?"

"No, no, no," said Del. "Quite the opposite. I now have much more solid information but there is a problem."

"So, tell me what it is. Maybe I can help," said Harry.

"I wish it were that simple, mate, but it seems anything to do with Tony Green becomes murky and dangerous. To think I didn't know that much about him not long ago." Del's face cleared of worry and he stood up. "Look, I'm sorry about this but I need a couple of hours to put some arrangements in place, then I can tell you what's going on. And you are going to want to know this, I promise you."

Harry knew when it was time to push and when you left people to it. He stuck out his hand and they said their goodbyes.

"I'll get back to you in the next few hours," said Del, who disappeared fast. His troubled expression showed he was a long way from his normal relaxed self.

CHAPTER 49

Martha took one look at Harry and knew he had something on his mind, even though he was attempting to cover his concern by clowning around with Julie.

She caught his attention. "Sorry to ambush you, but if I didn't know better, I would say you are wondering whether to keep something from me."

Harry was too shocked to deny her claim. "How on earth did you know that?"

"I've told you before, Harry. I've known you all my life and have learned all about your little tells. You might as well have a great big flashing sign on your head that spells out something is worrying you. It must be especially bad because you keep checking your fingernails."

"My fingernails . . ." Harry trailed off. He had no idea he had so many giveaways, but he should have known better than not telling Martha what was going on. She had a sixth sense about the truth and could see straight though lies. He considered bluffing it out then noticed she had her hands on her hips. She was getting annoyed and he didn't want to be in the firing line.

"Yes, you're right. It's all a bit of a puzzle and I don't quite know what it means so I thought it might help to wait and think about it. I was only hesitating because there's not actually anything to say."

There was a pause while Julie and Martha shared a look. Harry knew the phrase "idiot men" was running through their minds.

"You wondering whether to tell me nothing? That's a new one."

"Okay, that does sound strange. Let me explain. I saw my contact today, the guy who's helping us with Tony Green. He got in touch with me early this morning and said it was urgent we meet up.

"When I got there, he was acting a bit paranoid and left straight away because of the cameras. He took me to this odd little pub about five minutes from the station. It was empty apart from the landlord. My chap explained it was like some sort of safe house for ex-cops and the like.

"My contact was really agitated so I pushed him for more information. He said after contacting me this morning he had received a call, the contents of which were seriously worrying him. He said he needed to sort something out and said he would get back to me soon."

Harry rubbed his face and took a slug of the now lukewarm tea. "I've got no real idea what any of that means, so that's why I was wondering whether to mention anything or just let it develop."

"I can see your dilemma, Harry. Let's try and work it out as best we can," said Martha. "I'm assuming here that your contact is pretty tough — he's not going to run at the first sign of trouble?"

"I've never known anything to really bother him before and he's got no shortage of friends who can help him out."

"Right, that helps," said Martha. "What we have is a bloke who knows his way around and doesn't get scared the moment it gets tough. We also know that he's recently been asking around about Tony Green. Sorry to ask this, but did you put any pressure on him, maybe made him a little careless?"

"Nothing like that," said Harry. "He only ever asks around with people he knows and trusts, preferably ones who owe him a big favour."

"Fair enough and that is also quite important."

"Is it?" said Julie. "Between you and Harry I have to admit that I'm getting a bit lost here."

"Me too," said Harry.

Martha brushed her hair back. "Look, this is only speculation but let me have a go at interpreting this. I would bet that your contact, from the moment he left that pub, has gone on the run and one man who could make him do that is Tony Green — maybe not the man himself, but he's asked questions that are edging him closer than he wants to be."

Martha got up and paced around the kitchen, a sure sign she was thinking hard. "Okay. I take at least two conclusions from all this. It's not easy to get to Tony Green, as we and the Met can all testify, and even though he's rolling up his operation he still has his ear to the ground and knows when someone is sniffing around. The big thing we have to consider is: Have we run out of time? As you warned, Harry, if he's free to concentrate on us that isn't good news."

Harry was sorting through his pockets and didn't immediately answer. He was staring at a crumpled piece of paper, which he handed to Martha.

"What's this? It looks like a shopping list. Coco Pops . . . Is this for Betty?"

"That—" Harry tapped the paper — "is a very useful piece of information."

CHAPTER 50

"Some people are just born lucky . . . Others are born unlucky."

Tony Green was pacing up and down in front of the man shackled to the wall of a Victorian building. The room was in a poor state of repair and smelled of damp and mould. Thick dirty blankets and ripped ancient curtains covered the windows, acting as effective light and sound proofing.

"There's not a chance anyone will hear you," he told the sobbing figure hanging from his wrists. They were red raw from the pressure of taking his weight. "Now, where was I? Oh, that's right. Luck. You've always been a very lucky man, in my opinion. You got used to things going your way, but since you came into my world, things have changed."

Green closed the gap between them and wrinkled his nose. "You stink, you know that? You could do with a nice hot shower but there's no chance of that here. And like I said, you've run out of luck. You're like a man who buys a lottery ticket, discovers it has the winning numbers, then loses it."

Green reached out and patted the man on his cheek, gently, like they were old friends. "Now, what is interesting is that my luck has improved since I met you. It's like I have a secret power . . . I steal everyone else's luck."

He stepped back and reached for a bottle of zero-alcohol lager from a bucket filled with ice. He studied the beading on the bottle then took a long pull, staring knowingly at the man. "You'd like a drink of this, wouldn't you?"

The lifeless figure was too beyond exhaustion to respond.

"I'd love to offer you a bottle of this," said Green. "I've even got some with alcohol in them. Just say the word and you can have anything you want." He stepped closer and wafted the bottle under the shackled man's nose. Within seconds, his tongue was running round his parched lips.

"Well," said Green. "What's it going to be? Ice-cold beer or die of dehydration? Because I will leave you here if you don't tell me what I need to know."

Green took a few more swigs from his bottle. "Only the non-alcohol for me. I should imagine you could do with a drink of any description." He searched around in the bucket, finally picking out a bottle.

"See all that beading on the outside? That's what you get when it's properly cold. He mimed looking thoughtful, stroking his chin with his finger and thumb.

"I'm a reasonable man so here is what I'm going to do. I'm going to open a fresh bottle and give you a few sips. Just to wet your whistle."

He poured a tiny amount of chilled lager into the man's mouth, then two more, bigger mouthfuls.

"I'll tell you what you want to know. Just give me a bit more beer," said the victim, his voice hoarse.

Green poured half of the contents on the grubby floor. "The rest goes the same way if you don't start talking."

The man rocked his head from side to side in anguish.

"Are we ready to start?" Green rolled the cold bottle against the man's cheek.

"Show me the address again," said the man, his voice cracking but clear enough for Green to make him out.

Green showed him his phone screen.

"Yes, that's the address I gave," croaked the man. "I was told it has a basement which has helped you stay out of sight."

"There's no chance you got the address wrong? If you're not sure you need to tell me now before it's too late."

"No. I'm quite sure. I recognised the name and its location. I do quite a lot of business with some of the people who live in that area. I promise you, that's the truth."

A large shadow detached itself from the corner of room. "He's telling you the truth there. His body language is screaming for you to recognise that fact." As the man spoke, he gestured to the victim to emphasise his point.

"That's helpful. And I agree," said Green. "He just wants to get out of here alive." He pointed at the bucket of beer. "That is all yours now. I'm going to leave you here for a little while, about twenty minutes, then one of my men will release you."

He stepped closer and patted the man on his cheek once again. "Well done. That must have been hard for you. But it's all over now and soon you will be home."

Tears of relief rolled down the face of the hapless victim.

Green stepped away, then stopped and turned, pulling a small pistol from inside his jacket pocket. He adopted a firing stance, planting one foot in front of the other and, holding the gun double-handed, pointed unwaveringly at his captive's head.

"You didn't really think I was going to let you go, did you? You must have realised I detest loose ends, and since you've been digging around, you've started to attract too much attention. Which is bad news for you. But then again, I did tell you at the start that you were running out of luck."

Green sighted down the barrel, ignoring the way the victim's face had gone bright red and his eyes were bulging, and squeezed the trigger. In less than a single second, a hole appeared at the top of the captive's nose, just below his brow. The man slumped down, dead the moment the first blood appeared.

Even as Green turned away, a clean-up crew arrived and took the body down from the wall.

"Get that to Dorking tonight," said Green. "Remember, tonight is the last time we use that facility so make sure he gets a good send-off."

He watched as the body bag was zipped tight. He made an ironic gesture, miming a gun with his right hand.

"You always were a bit too clever for your own good, Del."

CHAPTER 51

"I can see an address at the bottom of this shopping list," said Martha. "And it's in posh part of London. Is this what I'm hoping it is?"

"It might be, it just might be," said Harry. "Del must have slipped it into my pocket when we both left that weird pub."

"This needs to be checked out urgently. Harry and Julie, get your arses over there now." Martha paced the small kitchen. "It could be the break we've been looking for."

Justin took the piece of paper from Martha. "I'll do a search for that address, it may produce some useful information."

"Good idea. Harry and Julie, I want you to call me the moment you get anything."

"Different topic, but I've got a question," said Julie. "Are you going to tell Lucy what we've found out or keep it to ourselves for now?"

"Tell me what?" said Lucy, who had just wandered into the kitchen.

Martha looked rueful. "I was just about to say we could never keep anything from you if you're going to be around here. We're pretty sure we have found the mansion Tony

Green has managed to get his grubby little hands on. Harry and Julie are heading over there now."

"You must know some serious people to have done that, Martha," said Lucy.

Martha smiled. "I do. Harry."

"I've said it before and I'll say it again, I'm glad he's on our side." Lucy pulled an envelope out of the briefcase she'd arrived with. She handed it to Martha, who drew out a picture. "What do you think?"

Martha's mouth dropped open. "Brilliant," she said. She held the print up for everyone to see. "This is the man I saw the other day.

"This is an AI-generated picture of what Tony Green looks like now, based on the information Martha gave me," said Lucy.

All eyes were glued to the image. Green's cheek bones were higher, his hair darker, but he still had that unmistakable sneer plastered his face.

Harry peered at the picture. "He's still an ugly old bastard. Money and plastic surgeons can't make a silk purse out of a sow's ear."

CHAPTER 52

An hour later, they were sitting in Harry's car with a clear view of the white stucco property that formed part of an enclave of similar houses.

"How much would one of these cost?" asked Julie after they had been parked for ten minutes. She had her seat pushed right back to accommodate her huge frame.

Harry grunted. "I could've bought one of these for about ten grand."

"What on earth stopped you, you daft plonker?" Julie looked incredulous.

"It was about fifty years ago," said Harry, "and you have to remember that was a lot of money back then. And I was worried about the neighbours, they might not have appreciated the type of company I keep." He cast a glance at Julie.

"Ooh, I'm sorry Harry," she said. "I just accidently crushed your crisps." She waved a packet of cheese and onion at him.

While they were bantering, two men in the back of a van with blacked-out windows had them under surveillance.

"I'll call the boss," said the older of the two.

A quarter of a mile away, Tony Green's phone rang.

"As expected. Harry and that big bird are keeping watch."

"That's good," said Green. "Now get out of there before they spot you."

As the pair drove away, the younger man looked frustrated.

"We could've taken them easily."

The older man never took his eyes off the road as he replied, "Those two have put more people in the ground than you've had hot dinners."

Within half an hour of the pair driving away, Tony Green walked past where they had been parked and headed towards Harry and Julie.

"Keep still," said Harry. "That's Green coming towards us. Let's see if he heads for the target."

A few minutes later, they watched him let himself in.

"That really could be him," said Harry.

"I agree," said Julie. "Let's report in."

CHAPTER 53

Tony Green dialled a number that was answered on the third ring.

"Expect things to start moving within the next twenty-four hours. They've taken the bait."

There was no reply. He hadn't expected one. If there had been even a murmur at the other end, he would have shut the operation down immediately. Yes, he had put a lot of effort into this but that counted for nothing if he himself fell into a trap.

He really wanted to kill Martha but he also wanted to live to enjoy the victory. Those irritating sidekicks of hers — Barry, no, Harry, and that creature of pure muscle, Julie — also deserved terminating, but he would settle for Martha. She was the brains who told the others what to do. He let his mind drift for a few moments more. *Don't kid yourself*, he thought. *You don't care who kills who.*

He'd enjoyed the sensation of having the two of them watching him as he walked past and climbed the short flight of steps to the front door. Inside the house, he'd been able to watch them through CCTV placed to cover the road outside. He knew they would be itching to get their hands on him.

Green rubbed his hands with barely suppressed glee as he thought about the next phases. Many a fine military expert has warned that a plan only survives first contact with the enemy. Well, in the humble opinion of Tony Green that was a trope that needed to be updated. First contact, in this instance, would see Martha's Army caught on the hop. It would be a bloodbath and would end with Green victorious and Martha in his control.

Even if there were a few problems, the very worst scenario would still see Martha fall into his hands. He wouldn't have a great deal of time with her but it would be enough. He picked up a small, fiendishly sharp knife from the table. Holding it up to the light, he tried to make out the edge of the blade.

If he was really lucky, this knife would be the last thing Martha laid eyes on. Starting at the top, he would cut one eye out, slice off her ears and then — his absolute pièce de résistance — using the razor-sharp blade, he would cut her stomach open and carefully remove her intestines, which she would place in her lap. Two tiny nicks would see her fluids leak into the cushions around her.

"I'm getting a hard on just thinking about this. But it's no more than she deserves. She has challenged the great Tony Green and that cannot be left unanswered." He didn't know it but in the last few weeks he had started to talk to himself.

He was pacing back and forwards in the larger of the two sitting rooms. He stopped his walking and cursed himself. "Stop being a moron," he told himself. "If you want your fun with Martha, you need to get your hands dirty first and capture the bitch. Which might be easier said than done. And there's no point getting hung up about killing her. If you get the chance, fantastic, but don't hold your breath."

She'd slipped through his fingers more times than he cared to admit. All this celebrating before he even had her was a mistake. He rang his man in charge of staking out her home.

"What's it like down there?"

"They're coming and going all the time. They're operating a ring defence, which means we are going to take losses. It depends how good the other lot are but we could lose half our people."

"I take it you are talking about the old pensioner and his sidekick?" said Green. "That's helpful to know. I'll be sure to keep some of our best people back for the assault on the house. That pair won't be coming quietly."

Green ended the call. His team was well prepared and armed with military grade weaponry. He didn't care how many of them were lost so long as they caught Martha. He had also long ago accepted that Harry and Julie were formidable opponents. He knew that no one on his team would stand a chance against them if they went up one to one.

Just in case they survived the attack — and he would bet they both might — he had a little side plan in place. He made a coffee as he ran through the options. He was as confident as he could be that he had the variables covered by the right people. People who would see the job through.

He was expecting a call from one of them very soon.

CHAPTER 54

Harry hated having to pay so much to drive in London. Ultra-low this, congestion charge that, and then paying to park. On top of it all, he found it especially irritating operating the new parking machines. His thick fingers were not designed for delicate keypad operations and he hated all the different companies.

"Why can't it just be Ringo all the time?" he said as he attempted to open the right app.

"Harry," said Julie.

He didn't hear her, he was concentrating so hard.

"Harry," she said, louder this time.

"Uhhh," he said.

"Harry, will you just listen to me?" She prodded him in the ribs to gain his attention.

"I am trying to pay this stupid car parking charge. What happened to good old cash. It's a deliberate thing to upset us older people."

"When you've finished rabble-rousing for the OAPs, I have some information that might interest you."

"What's that?" Harry tapped furiously at his phone to absolutely no effect.

"I've paid," said Julie. "We can go when you want."

"You might have said," he announced, causing Julie to tap her head against the dashboard.

Gathering his pride, he pulled away from the kerb.

"Watch out," said Julie. "It's a twenty mile an hour zone here."

"Bloody zones. When I was your age, we could pull wheelies around here."

"Pah!" said Julie. "When you were my age, you were in a horse and cart."

Arriving back in Dulwich, they walked back into Martha's house, where she, Justin and Lucy were waiting.

"Shall I go first?" said Justin. "Get my stuff out of the way. I picked up a lot of information, but most of it is complicated legal gobbledygook. The mansion, which is technically owned by a holding company in Knightsbridge, is actually at the centre of one of the most complicated ownership schemes I've ever encountered.

"I can track the property and its various holding companies but that tells you nothing at all about who actually owns it."

There were moans all around and Justin waited for the noise to die down a bit. "Are you already for the last bit?" he asked. "Always save your best bit for the end. It turns out there is a very strong Russian connection to this property. It seems the Russian owners were turfed out along with many others when the British Government started imposing penalties on individuals to make them pay for the war in the Ukraine. I expect you are all hoping it is someone famous like Abramovich or the like, but it is in fact some people that we've never heard of. But, by all accounts, a nasty bunch."

"That's useful, thanks, Justin. Is that as far as you can go in your research?"

"No it's not. Like I said, best last. This house holds a lot of secrets. It's said to have one of the most complicated underground set of rooms in London which includes parking, cinema, swimming pool and spa area. It's like an iceberg, there's far more below ground than above.

"It was started about twenty years ago and weirdly the council have no records or plans for the development."

Martha shook her head. "Isn't it unbelievable that secret building projects are being run by the Russians in London? No wonder Tony Green is using this building. Everything about the mansion and Green himself makes them very well matched." She turned to Harry. "Just a thought — I wonder how your contact got this address? Have you heard from him since your meeting?"

"I've sent him a couple of messages, but so far have heard nothing," said Harry. "He seemed a little agitated when he was in the pub and his involvement in this had stirred things up a bit more than he wanted, so he was disappearing. I've only ever known him do this once before. Shows how worried he is. And as we all know, he has always been careful. Even though he can call on some serious help he stays out of trouble before it gets him."

"That is interesting," said Martha. "The one man we all know who can cause that sort of reaction is Tony Green."

She sat down, deep in thought. "Okay, this is how I see it," she said after a short pause. "We have found him and his hideout. The question is — what do we do next? Do we go in ourselves with little intel on what we will run into or pass this on to Paula Charteris?"

"Can I be the first to answer that?" said Julie.

"Go ahead," said Martha, certain that her answer would be that they should go in with guns blazing.

"I think we should leave it to the police," said Julie, to Martha's total surprise.

"I really expected you to want to go in punching."

"That may be my usual response, I admit," said the big woman. "But Tony Green never fights fair. For all we know this is some elaborate plan to trick us into a trap he's got set up. It does seem that it has been a bit too easy that we have found him, especially as he is meant to be the master of shadows. I say leave it to the special weapons and training lot. They can look after themselves if it gets crazy."

"I agree with Julie," said Harry. "He really is a slippery little eel. If that wasn't enough, I think you have no choice but to tell Charteris about this. He's their most wanted criminal and he's already run rings round the Met. I seriously think that if you held this information back, they'd lock you up and throw away the key. Hell, they'd lock all of us up."

"I think both of you are exactly right. We leave this one to the specialists," said Martha. "But when I talk to Paula Charteris I'll ask if there's any role we can play. Even if it's just as observers, because I wouldn't mind seeing that bastard led away in handcuffs."

"Don't worry about us taking part," said Harry waving to include Julie. "I think we would be about as welcome as a fart in a lift. But you are the exception to the rule. You're one of them . . ."

He stopped and raised an eyebrow. "When I said that, I should have said you're one of the good ones. You should just concentrate on yourself. You need to be there so you can be welcomed back by your mates in the Met."

"My mates in the Met? Now I've heard it all," said Martha. "Lucky, I know you're pulling my leg. But you're right, I need to keep you two low profile and I will try to be there . . . but only out of interest. My bet is that weird woman from MI5, the one who hates me even though we've never really talked, won't let me within half a mile of any operation."

"How can this woman keep you out of a police raid?" asked Julie.

"Easy," said Martha. "It won't be a police raid. It's supposed to be a joint police/MI5 operation but the spooks are in charge. What they say goes — even overruling the Commissioner herself. I hear they even have their own special ops team to get involved in any shooting."

"No good ever came out of the spooks being in charge," said Harry. "It was your dad who first told me that, Martha, and he has been proven right over and over."

"Thanks for those words of wisdom, Harry," said Martha. "You're right as always. Now, unless anyone has anything to add, I need to dig out that number she gave me."

CHAPTER 55

"I was almost too clever for my own good there," said Martha. "When the Commissioner gave me her number, she told me not to list it under something obvious like Paula."

"So what did you use?" asked Julie.

"I picked PC Bloggs, so that her initials were hidden in the abbreviation for police constable. Naturally, the first time I need it, I can't remember how I listed it in the phone memory.

"You've no idea how much that cheers me up, it's exactly the sort of thing I do," said Julie.

Martha raised an eyebrow before staring at her handset as if it was somehow trying to trick her, before holding up the device to prove that she had indeed finally retrieved the correct number.

"Only a handful of people have this." She placed the phone on the table in front of her. "The Commissioner said this number will allow me to reach her at any time, day or night. Apparently, it isn't recorded anywhere within the Met. It all sounds a bit old-school, if I'm honest. Even worse, it's like when my dad was around, treating rules as if they only apply to other people. But that's the way she wants things done, so who am I to moan about it? The only thing I want is to get through to her as quickly as possible."

She picked the phone up. "Unless anyone has any last-minute observations, I'm going to call now."

Harry looked around, thinking that over the years this kitchen had been used for everything from an impromptu command and control centre to a warm space to enjoy the company of friends over plentiful supplies of tea. And several wonderful birthday parties. His eyes narrowed as he thought of the dark shadow hanging over all their lives and threatening their future.

"I think I can speak for all of us when I say that the quicker we get on with this, the better." His eyes glittered the way Martha had seen them do several times before . . . He was putting himself on a war footing, ready for the fight that was almost upon them. It reminded her like a punch to the gut that Green could strike at any moment.

Martha forced herself to stop being distracted and to focus on the job in hand. Before picking up the phone again, she had one more question for them.

"Even though the Commissioner promised this number would reach her straight away, my guess is that I'm sure to be asked to leave a message. Any thoughts on what I should say?"

"Tell her you have news and you need to meet immediately," said Justin. "Keep it simple with as little detail as possible. Make her call you back to find out what you want."

"What he said," said Julie and Harry almost simultaneously.

"Good, because that's exactly what I'm thinking too," said Martha. "I can tell her we have to meet. She'll obviously know it's about Tony Green but I won't give her any clues. I'll insist we meet face to face."

"How much do you think we can trust her?" said Harry.

"I wish I knew but she's a difficult woman to read. I can never tell what she's thinking. Ordinarily, I wouldn't trust her any further than I could throw her. But this is different

. . . given that she is the Commissioner I don't see how she can do anything other than take our information and do something about it. I don't think she can dare do anything else. It's the same sort of discussion we just had.

"But I have been thinking about this a lot — if she is part of the enemy team, then us discovering Green's hideout might just make her, and her associates, get a little jumpy. They might decide to attack us straight away. Which means, Harry and Julie, it's a good thing that we have Lucy on board and have ratcheted up security as high as we can take it."

"Exactly," said Harry. "We have the new protocols in place. The point is, you won't even notice that they are in place but if you have any questions then just ask me."

"How are you getting on with having two of her people in the house?"

Martha looked around. "You know, I'd forgotten about that. We tried it with two extra people and everyone agreed it was just too crowded. Lucy suggested a compromise of one extra person and she's sticking to the upstairs landing. I'm not completely convinced but I'm willing to give it a go. For now."

Justin looked up from his computer screen. "Hang on, guys, can I just add to what I have already found out about the mansion?"

Harry and Julie exchanged a brief look. This could be interesting.

"Please do," said Martha.

"As I mentioned, the house belongs to a Russian oligarch, who was among a load of Putin supporters booted out after Russia invaded Ukraine. He'd owned it for a very long time and apparently spent a fortune on renovations including a huge basement area. I have now found out that it was done about twenty years ago so details are sketchy. But there were newspaper reports that neighbours complained about the scale of the works. They say it lasted for a couple of years so it must have been a big deal. I have put in some special requests for more information."

Harry and Julie, for two people who maintained they could never not vote Labour, were gazing around in admiration. Martha shrugged but kept quiet. To be fair, very few people had ever visited a house like this so a little bit of gawking was hardly amiss.

"I found an article in the *Financial Times* that said that he had somehow managed to retain ownership despite supposedly being persona non grata. The suggestion was that he had been very generous with his bribes, which stopped anyone looking too closely at the current arrangements.

"The other standout is that the house Green is using is in a block of six properties and unusually I can find no trace of who the other five belong to, just the names of holding companies, which appear to have been dormant since the purchase of the remaining five houses — shortly after the oligarch bought his. It's almost as though they had one purpose only . . . buying one of the other five houses and, once that was complete, there has been no further activity.

"I should add that this type of thing is not a rare occurrence. But only certain groups of people do it like this because the seemingly excessive secrecy can attract interest. For most people, that would be counterproductive.

"Now, this is just a guess on my part but so much secrecy suggests our Russian friend is both determined to have privacy at all costs — and is probably extremely confident that his cybersecurity is top notch. Which it may be if he has connections to the Russian military."

Martha had been listening closely. "Justin, thank you so much. And what you don't say is that while he may have military grade tech, you still seem to have found your way through."

"To be honest, some of the stuff you hear about brilliant government technology is talked up to deter people from having a go," said Justin. "To be honest I found it quite straightforward. I've been going slow to make sure I cover our tracks — I didn't want to add a visit from Russian security services to our woes."

"Can you keep digging?" said Martha. "At least without attracting unwelcome attention. From what you've just told us, I have the strongest sense — if you can forgive the pun — that the information you are trying to dig up on the basement developments could really help us."

She didn't wait for an answer. Justin was one of those people who didn't feel the need to fill a silence. It was one of the reasons Harry liked him since he shared the same attitude. Let other people do the talking.

"Right," said Martha. "I'm going to call that number now. I'll go into the front room so I'll see you all later."

"I do like it when you come over all boss like," said Julie grinning as Martha left the kitchen.

Sitting down on the settee, Martha made the call, listening patiently as the number rang for a surprisingly long time. The ringing tone finally ended, followed by a loud click then a moment of silence.

The Commissioner's voice followed. "Please leave your message. This service is checked constantly."

Martha left her message and ended the call. Sitting back in her comfortable chair, she had the creeping sensation that something was wrong, but she didn't know what. She didn't want the others to see her like this, worried and anxious. With a supreme effort of will, she put on a bright smile and returned to the kitchen.

"I knew it," she told them. "It was a case of leaving a message. Let's see how long she takes to call." She didn't stop smiling.

Harry offered to make her a fresh cup of tea.

"Actually, I'm going to say no, I'm going to use this time to run the events of the day through my mind while it's all quiet. I'll be in my room, but only for a short while. Give me twenty minutes."

As she climbed the stairs towards her bedroom, she grimaced. She was sure that Harry had spotted her turmoil. He always had been able to read her like a book, no matter how well she thought she was disguising her thoughts or moods.

Ordinarily, she accepted Harry's mind-reading ability as just one of his skills but this time she wasn't sure what it was she was worried about. She wouldn't keep this from the others, at least not for long. But right now, she didn't want to introduce a new problem without having some sort of concrete proof. Just tossing it in without a full explanation was a recipe for disaster.

But try as she might, she couldn't ditch a feeling of foreboding that made her think of death. It was almost overwhelming and she started to cry, which astonished her. Martha never cried — only at her mum's funeral and the safe return of Betty from the hands of her kidnappers. For a moment, a feeling of panic grew and she had a sudden vision of Julie and Harry lying on the ground, blood gushing everywhere.

She couldn't stand it if something happened to them. She was certain they would do anything to save her, but would she be able to do the same . . . even sacrificing her own life?

Then she thought of Betty. Would she ever be able to forgive her mother for sacrificing her own life to try and save her friends?

She put her head in her hands and wept bitter, salty tears, her shoulders heaving from the emotion.

There was a knock on the door and Harry walked in, not waiting for the invite. Silently, he crossed the room and trapped her in a big bear hug that took her breath away. Slowly, he let go and, holding both shoulders, just looked at her. In that moment, it was as though some sort of positive mental transfer had taken place. Whatever it was she already felt better.

"No one is getting killed today, no one is getting hurt today . . . at least not on our side of the game," said Harry.

His words acted like a balm. She rubbed her hands and realised she had been sweating. She hoped there was time for a shower and a fresh change of clothes.

"How do you do it, Harry? How do you know when I need you?"

"Because you try so hard to be care free that it stands out a mile."

"Don't ever tell me that if you can read my reaction to going out on a date," she said.

"Why go on dates when you've got Justin?"

"I know you're only saying this to give my racing thoughts a rest but I don't mind. Justin and I have had a long talk and after this is all over we have decided to get back together, which has made us both happy." She smiled.

"I think that's a very good idea for you and Betty and I'm happy for you," said Harry, still holding her shoulders. "Now, you need to tidy up and come back and talk to the others. How long do you think it'll be before you get a call back?"

"The Commissioner said when she handed me her card that, and I quote, 'In the unlikely event you get my voice-mail, then expect to hear from me within thirty minutes.' It's been six minutes since I called so not long to go."

Martha gave Harry a gentle hug, whispering "thank you" in his ear and headed towards the bathroom to wash her face.

Walking back into the kitchen, and with two minutes to go before the unofficial deadline, her phone rang.

It was the Commissioner.

"I gather you have some news for me. Well, not to be outdone, I have some news for you. Shall I go first?"

CHAPTER 56

Martha nodded then remembered to talk.

"Please go ahead. Just so you know, I have Julie and Harry here, listening in."

"That's fine," said Paula. "I know you don't go very far without one of those two. Before I tell you what's happened, let me give you some of the back story. As you know, the Met and MI5 have set up a joint task force to investigate Tony Green and his operation. I know there are issues around that as far as you're concerned and we will have to come back to those later.

"What you probably aren't aware of is that the remit for the task force has changed. Before, it was essentially a one-off designed specifically with Green in mind but that has changed, quite significantly.

"Basically, the new Home Secretary heard about it and liked the idea. His people want to expand it into a kind of super task force that can tackle anything. They're envisaging it as Special Forces team, armed with the latest weapons and technology to tackle the 'scourge' — the Minister's words — of crime."

"Sorry to interrupt, ma'am," said Martha. "But my understanding is that the military cannot get involved in domestic crime issues."

"It's complicated," said the Commissioner. "Ordinarily, the army would not be called into a domestic crime incident. But if it was seen as critical to national security, they could be. If that wasn't enough, the MI5 woman who set up and runs the squad — and I can't tell you who she is — pulled a clever stroke. She staffed it with former military people, sitting alongside some of our best police officers. After a bit of retraining, she can now claim to be 'launch ready' to meet any threat from Green, to anti-terror and international organised crime. She claims she can have a team ready to go at a moment's notice."

"Forgive me again, but this sounds an awful lot like the SAS," said Martha.

"It is," said the Commissioner. "The difference is that this unit can call on the services of the Home Secretary's spin doctors. By the time they'd finished, it sounded like some sort of cross between *Thunderbirds*, *James Bond* and some super top-secret unit no one has ever heard of.

"The Home Secretary is delighted. Says it's an absolute vote winner and the word is that he's trying to launch it in a way that outflanks the Prime Minister himself. Apparently, he fancies a little run at the top job and intends to take full credit for setting this up."

Butterflies swooped in Martha's stomach, rekindling her sense of concern. "I take it this is going to have an impact on the pursuit of Tony Green?"

"Yes, but I don't think it is a negative one. From today we will still have a dedicated unit hunting him. If they find him, they can launch an operation, still under MI5 control but also leaving a deputy position open for a senior police officer with relevant experience of fighting high-level crime. In addition, you will still be able to call on the help of the SAS if you need it."

Martha didn't answer at first. Alarm bells were ringing but she was desperate not to let it show.

"Are you still on the line, Martha?" asked the Commissioner.

"Apologies, ma'am. That all sounds good to me. It keeps the politicians happy and still leaves you able to act as you see fit. I do have one question, if I may?"

"Go ahead."

"Given that this is a new unit, can I repeat my request to be directly involved?"

"Your enthusiasm is noted. I will pass this to the relevant people. As previously stated, I intend to keep you in the loop. Which reminds me, we started this conversation with a promise by me that I had something new on Green. MI5 has confirmed evidence that our man is back in London. The suggestion is he came in on a flight from South America, although it is not known which country he came from."

"Thanks for that, ma'am," said Martha. "I was going to tell you something similar with a bit more information."

She heard a sharp intake of breath down the line then the Commissioner spoke again, apparently as unflappable as before. "Please go on."

"I can confirm that he's back. I also have a location for where he may be hiding out and a possible illustration of what he looks like now."

The silence at the other end was considerably longer. Then the Commissioner spoke again. "How long will it take you to get to Scotland Yard?"

"I can be there in ninety minutes at most. A lot less depending on the journey," said Martha.

"Get here." The Commissioner cut the line.

CHAPTER 57

Martha rushed upstairs to change. She decided to stick to civilian clothes. By the time she got downstairs, there was the usual debate about the fastest way into town, which Justin ended.

"I've checked all routes and the best way right this moment is train to Victoria from West Dulwich and then the District line to Westminster. The train goes in ten minutes. You'll have plenty of time."

"If I give her a lift," said Harry.

A little under an hour since the Commissioner had ended the call, Martha arrived at Scotland Yard. Within minutes of reporting in she had been collected from front reception and escorted to Paula Charteris's office.

As before, it was a hive of activity but to her surprise, she didn't recognise anyone there.

Her escort lightly touched her on the arm. "The Commissioner will be here in ten minutes. Do you need anything?"

She did. She had once gone for a job interview that had meant getting on the tube. Somewhere between departure and arrival, she had picked up a soot-coloured smudge right across her forehead, which she only spotted using the bathroom at the end of the interview.

Since then, Martha had gone to great pains to check her appearance before an appointment whenever the opportunity presented itself. When she came out of the ladies, she found her escort waiting. She was not going to be left loose up here, which was reinforced by the next words from her escort. "If you follow me, we can sit at my workstation while you wait. I've got a couple of chairs."

No bottled mineral water and comfortable settee this time, thought Martha. That sense of apprehension was back again. It was giving her a dull ache in the stomach.

It was twenty minutes before Paula Charteris arrived. She went straight into her office, leaving Martha to wait another fifteen minutes sitting on a very uncomfortable seat. With her right leg starting to feel numb, she was finally called in.

She put on her best cheerful face, determined not to show the slightest irritation at the way she had been treated, and walked into the main office to find the Commissioner sitting at her desk. There was no one else present, which surprised her. Paula Charteris was famous for being ultra-cautious and always spoke to people with one of her underlings present, who would be required to take notes.

"Sit down, Martha." She indicated the chair in front of her desk. For a moment, she looked so intently at Martha that she had the distinct impression she was being judged in some way.

The Commissioner appeared to reach a decision. She leaned forward. "What I'm about to tell you must remain strictly confidential. Not a word of this can escape this office. When you hear what I tell you, you will understand the reasons why this is essential."

Martha shifted in her seat. She hadn't been expecting this.

"After you made your request to be placed with the new unit tracking Tony Green, I passed that on with my blessing. In all the circumstances, I couldn't see a problem — especially given how much information you have been able to supply. Everything we have is down to you.

"To my utter amazement, I received a call from the Home Secretary's senior Special Adviser. I was told in no uncertain terms that you remained someone of interest to MI5 and therefore would not be trusted. He said that MI5 was totally in charge and had the full authority and backing of the Minister.

"I was then informed — off the record, of course — that I would be jeopardising my career if I continued to support you."

She stopped and looked at Martha, who for once was speechless.

"I imagine you can now see why I want this kept confidential. But having said that, I'm not throwing in the towel. That bloody man threatened me for doing my job and I don't take kindly to it. We can't have men bullying women just because they think they can get away with it. I won't have that at all. It does, however, make me wonder whether someone has got to him — that someone being Green.

"Let's see how things pan out in the next twenty-four hours. I'm betting that an opportunity will emerge to somehow get you involved. I'm not promising a ringside seat but it's better than peering in from the outside."

Martha nodded thoughtfully at this information.

"On the phone you mentioned that you had some information to share with me," said the Commissioner.

"I do. We've received multiple confirmations of the mansion that Green is located in. Harry and Julie have also seen Green enter the premises. We have an inkling of what he's up to, and that is liquidating all his UK assets, ready to leave the country within the next couple of weeks.

"As we've suspected all along, Green has used a plastic surgeon, which has changed his appearance successfully. I have an AI-enhanced picture of what he looks like now, which I can leave with you."

The Commissioner leaned back in her chair. "That's a lot of information and far better than I could have hoped for. Well done, Martha."

Martha stood up. "Thank you, ma'am. Shall I wait to hear from you?"

"Yes, and only me. No one else, no matter their rank. I'm not sure who to trust at the moment."

It took supreme effort for Martha to stop herself running out of the door. Events were speeding up. She wanted to get home. That feeling of peril was building and she was certain that the threat of danger towards her and everyone close to her was about to become very real.

CHAPTER 58

The Special Firearms Unit had been set up within weeks of the suicide bombers attacking the London Underground. As well as firearms training, they were all skilled medics and communications experts. The medical expertise was essential in situations where the unit was first on the scene, and saved many lives while waiting for paramedic responders.

Comprising twenty people on active duty and twenty more who could be deployed if they were needed, the unit took pride in responding within minutes to any situation. So when they received the command to get ready for action in the next twenty-four hours they all shrugged. Twenty-four hours was a walk in the park — say twenty-four minutes and that might be pressure.

Unaware of this, Martha made it back to Dulwich as fast as she could go. She was so full of adrenaline that she sprinted home from West Dulwich Station to Idmiston Road.

Julie was alone in the kitchen making herself toast. "You want some?"

Martha was about to say no then stopped herself. "That's not a bad idea. I could do with something simple." She did a double take. "Where are Harry and Justin? They're normally first in the queue if anyone is making toast."

"They've gone to get Betty. Harry wants her home a bit earlier so she doesn't get caught up in the home time rush." She finished buttering her toast and ate it in three huge bites, placing a fresh couple of slices in the toaster as she did so. Martha buttered her own toast and took a smaller bite.

Betty walked in with Harry and Justin. "Toast. Can I have some? It's not dinner for ages yet."

She prepared the toast while looking at Harry. The faintest of nods showed he had something to say. First, she had to settle Betty down.

"When you've had your toast, do you want to watch TV for a bit or do your homework?" asked Martha.

"I'd like to look at my iPad, please."

"And you know what my answer is going to be, don't you?"

"Homework first, then iPad, because I don't want to ruin my life . . . Okay then. Can I have a glass of water and watch TV? Then I'll do my homework."

The exchange between mother and daughter had lightened the mood a little. There was no doubt that living with the knowledge that you were a target for a very dangerous man made for a more pressurised existence, but Martha had always made it clear she would not be forced out of her house. An equally important red line was that Betty should remain completely oblivious to what was going on around her.

This was easier said than done. Betty was every bit as smart as her mum and was wise beyond her years. Martha bitterly regretted that part of this maturity was because not only had she been kidnapped by enemies of her father, but they had bungled their plan and murdered her grandmother.

The little girl had shown no signs at all of any reaction but she also shared another trait with her mother — she was one tough cookie. No one should have to go through such an ordeal . . . let alone a little girl. She and Justin had agreed that Betty have a session every two weeks with a psychologist. After the first session, the psychologist had explained that Betty had built a mental force field around herself: *"You were right to say she's tough. There may be trouble in the short term but I think the extraordinary courage she has shown already will stand her in good stead when she's ready to deal with this."*

Martha looked at her daughter drinking her water. Powerful emotions of fear and pride ran through her. At that moment, all other issues were swept to one side. She would do anything for Betty, literally anything.

If she'd had eyes in the back of her head, she'd have seen Harry looking at them both, his eyes wet and shiny. Julie reached out and squeezed his bicep. He looked down at the floor then took a deep breath. "Get a grip, old man," he told himself.

Justin and Betty headed into the front room and turned the TV on.

"Harry, Julie and I will be in the kitchen if you need anything. Don't open the door without letting us know. You be good, you two," Martha said, as she closed the door quietly behind her and looked up the stairs to Lucy's security guard. When she returned to the kitchen, she turned to Harry. "What have you got for us?"

"As you know, Tony Green is a slippery little git. Normally, in a situation like this all sorts of people know that something is going to happen. There are weapons suppliers, transport specialists, clean-up crews and surveillance teams, internet experts . . . the list could go on.

"But the point is with all these people a little bit will escape and if you know the right places to ask around you can find out what's going on. I'm not saying it's easy, but it can be done.

"So, Mr Clever Dick Green seems to have avoided all of that. I can't get a sniff of anything, which is a pain in the backside. But that's all it is. At the end of the day, we know he is going to attack us. The best thing we can do is be ready. From right now we should expect him any time, so at least we won't get caught with our trousers down if he turns up. This also gives us a small advantage. He won't be expecting us to be waiting to give him a bloody nose."

"Bring it on," said Julie. At these moments, when she was pumped up and ready to fight, Martha thought her friend looked stunning. Terrifying but amazing.

She had been intending to tell them all about her unspecified doubts but now wasn't the appropriate moment. She didn't want to inject a negative feeling into the discussion. Harry was pumped and ready.

"I've discussed this with Lucy and she agrees," he said. "She's got some big bodyguarding job on but will be here later. She's leaving all her people here. Which is good." Harry's forehead creased, a sure sign that he was concerned. "I also need to let you know about something which I can't quite get my head round. Four of my team suddenly stepped down. They claimed it was for personal reasons. Now, I might have gone along with that if it was one person, or even two, but this was four people all suddenly leaving.

"I know one of the four pretty well and I got hold of him. He didn't want to talk at first but he owes me a lot of favours. He said they all suddenly came under pressure from the police. They were left in no doubt that staying on this job with me would have a seriously negative effect on their future health. My man said he had no doubt they meant it."

"I don't get that, Harry," said Julie. "The police are always pulling the old 'It's about to get worse' routine. Why are your guys suddenly getting worried about it?"

"I am the police," said Martha, "and I can confirm that that is precisely what happens. I mean, you're hardly going to tell some snot-rag that they'd best keep schtum and everything will be all right. Where are the four now, Harry?"

"That's what is really bothering me. Since speaking to them they've vanished. Not a trace."

"How important are these four to your plans?" said Martha.

"Well, that's the funny bit. They're not essential really, except in one way. The news has gone round super-fast, meaning everyone has heard and everyone is worried. Which reminds me of one little detail. Apparently, the officers who turned up at their home were in full dress uniform. I have no idea why."

"I do," said Julie. All eyes switched to her. "They wanted to make as big a splash as possible so no one could miss them."

Martha patted her on the arm. She was often all jokes, but occasionally she said something serious, and invaluable.

"Well done, Julie. The next question is, who do we all know who likes grand gestures?"

"Tony Green," came the answer.

"My third question is why?"

This time there was no response. Martha didn't delay. "Tony Green is an old-school conman who likes to distract attention from what he's doing. Getting people to dress up is a sure way to make your audience look in the opposite direction. It would be good to find out what he's really up to.

"If nothing else, it's a strong reminder that nothing is ever the way it seems where that man is concerned. Keep it at the back of your mind — it may make more sense later."

Her phone beeped with a message. It was the Commissioner.

CHAPTER 59

Paula Charteris answered on the first ring.

"I can get you in the control room," said Charteris. "It's the best I can do. Do you want to take it?"

"Yes please. What do I need to do?"

"I'm glad you accepted the proposal. You have no idea of what it took to get you that. You'll be working alongside the command team of the Special Firearms Unit, which will be operating out of Wellington Barracks.

"They're in the process of setting up the operation now with the intention of going into that address you gave me tomorrow evening. Of course, that could all change so you need to report to Wellington Barracks at 10 a.m. tomorrow and ask to speak to Commander Ian Walker. He'll run you through what you can and can't do. Good luck, Martha. We'll speak again once this is all over — for better or worse."

Martha replied with a thank you but the connection had already ended.

"How much of that did you all get?" Martha asked her team. She'd had her phone on loudspeaker and they all indicated they'd heard.

"Once I get inside the barracks, I doubt I will be able to talk to you again until it is all over," said Martha.

"Just a thought," said Harry. "You won't be able to contact us but will we be able to send you a text? I'm wondering what we do if we pick up something important."

"I think you just have to try. I really can't see what else you can do." She picked up her mug of tea and took a sip. Putting it down, she froze. The other two went quiet — they'd seen this before. Martha was piecing together random thoughts floating around in her brain.

"If you wanted to distract people about an attack here in Dulwich, then the Special Firearms Unit assaulting a building in central London would be a good way of doing it," said Martha.

"But that would imply that Green had enough influence to arrange it all." Harry looked concerned.

"You're starting to think what I'm thinking, Harry," said Martha. "Could it be that we've been spoon-fed all the information? Does this mean that we've heard exactly what we expected to be told?" She rubbed her eyes, a bad habit that emerged when she felt stressed. "The problem is that you can drive yourself mad with all this," she went on. "You start challenging everything and before long you disappear down the rabbit hole.

"But look at the way we've received the information — we start off strongly suspecting that Green has very senior people at the Met under his control . . . and suddenly I'm flavour of the month with Paula Charteris. Maybe that's a coincidence or maybe that's Green looking to stoke our worries. No wonder we start to feel paranoid. And what about your contact, Harry, and the four missing men? It's very convenient of them to disappear. And Lucy — where has she gone? Why is it she has to do a bodyguard job on her own?"

Julie broke the silence. "I may not be the sharpest knife in the box but if it looks like a duck—"

"What?" said Harry. "What looks like a duck?"

"Never mind that," said Julie. "Regardless of who turns out to have got this right, I vote we get fully tooled up right away and stay like that. I know Martha is bothered about us having guns around Betty, but we need to make sure we can stay safe."

CHAPTER 60

Martha knew how much military types hated it when people displayed poor timekeeping so had been careful to turn up fifteen minutes early for her meeting with Commander Walker. She'd been shown into a small spartan waiting area comprising of four cheap plastic office chairs and a portrait of the King. She'd been left to her own devices without a word other than, "Wait here." If it was intended to undermine her, she had to admit it was having an effect. But only when she allowed it to. By the time the fifteen minutes was up, she was in control of her emotions.

Five more minutes and the Commander turned up. He was tall, straight-backed and wearing what she always thought of as classic army fatigues. He was also apologetic.

"Sorry to keep you waiting. The last meeting overran." He led her down a flight of steps, along a broad corridor and into what was clearly a command centre with a large screen on one wall and smaller screens on desks around the room.

"This is where you will be observing the operation from. We've been able to tap into feeds covering every inch of the target property and have been watching since last night." As he spoke, Walker gestured round the room, taking in the different feeds, then looked back at Martha. "I gather it's down to you that we have this address, or at any rate, someone who is working with you. It would be very helpful if we could meet this person and ask questions."

Martha had anticipated being asked exactly this. "I'm sorry, but a lot of lives are at risk here. Just knowing who my source is could put them — and their families — at risk. I understand this must be frustrating for you, but it's how it has to be."

If Walker was irritated by this response, he didn't show it. "That's not unreasonable," he said. "Do you think it's possible your contact will be able to provide more information to you?"

"We're hoping so," said Martha. "If I do get anything, then you will be the first to know."

"Naturally," said the Commander, still keeping his tone quite neutral. He walked to one of the desks and gestured at it. "You will be working from here, helping us to monitor the screens. If you do spot our target, don't worry about shouting out, he won't be able to hear you."

She couldn't tell if he was being sarcastic and took the lead from him by remaining unperturbed. Instead, she asked a question of her own. "Have you seen any activity at the property yet?"

"Not really. There's a couple of pictures on your desk of two youngish men who turned up late afternoon yesterday. MI5 has identified them as a pair of jobbing IT experts normally for hire on the dark web. They haven't been out yet. Have a look and see if they mean anything to you.

"Otherwise, we have managed to obtain observation posts around the target property. There was no sign of life last night or this morning. Given that we know at least two were in there, it suggests the basement area is in use or we'd have spotted some activity.

"Thanks to your information, we are assuming that below ground is quite substantial so there could be a lot of people there."

"I agree with you," said Martha. "As I understand it, some of these underground spaces are very large — especially if they were among the first to be dug out before councils started getting tougher about what you could do. This development may have been one of the first in London."

Walker gave her an appraising look. "That is interesting to know. I think we need to assume you're right. Better that than finding ourselves completely outgunned down there."

Martha sat at her desk. She looked carefully at the pictures but knew straight away she had no idea who the men were. Putting them back down, she looked at the feed on her screen. It was in colour and showed a window opening to the ground floor.

She resisted sighing but this was going to be a long day of playing the waiting game. She knew she had to show willing but there really were better things she could be doing with her time.

About an hour later, Walker came over to talk to her again. "I forgot to mention the coffee arrangements. In a short while, someone will come to take your order for drinks and food. Sort out the times with them. I will offer one bit of advice. Avoid the egg sandwich at all costs and order slightly more than you need. And the toilets are by the door you came in."

Martha saw the chance to ask questions of her own. "I was told yesterday that you were thinking of going in at about 5 p.m. Is that still the case?"

"You'll know when it happens," was all he said.

Seeing he was about to walk off, she quickly spoke. "If I get more information, can my contact reach me by sending a message?"

He seemed to freeze then nodded and walked away.

CHAPTER 61

Join the army and see the world. That definitely wasn't happening in Martha's case. Her highlight of the day so far was deciding to choose a ham and tomato sandwich for her lunch. She'd eaten half along with a lukewarm cup of tea diluted with too much milk. She decided to wait a little while longer before having the second half.

This momentous decision made, she went back to studying a window that probably hadn't been opened in many a year. While she was bored, she didn't allow what was happening to stress her out. "Never show you're hurting" was another Harry message drummed in to her from an early age.

Her phone pinged quietly with an incoming message. Walker swung round in his chair to watch her while she read it.

I should be getting something at 5 p.m. H.

Martha got up and headed over to Walker, to whom she handed over the phone with the message on screen.

His reaction surprised her. "Put a half-hour delay on the op," he told the woman sitting at the desk next to his. She whispered into a phone and passed the message on.

Martha had seen enough to more or less work out what had happened but was happy to wait for the Commander to fill in the gaps.

"We're going in at 5.15 p.m. now thanks to your information. I'd hate to go half an hour earlier and run into a problem we could have avoided. No clues as to what you might be getting?"

"I wish," said Martha. She hesitated but then her curiosity got the better of her. "I take it you're waiting for rush hour so that there are a few more people and vehicles around. What time are you sending the team over?"

"The strike team are already in place," said Walker. "We have twenty people altogether but half will be backup and the primary team will crack the door and spread around the building."

"It must take a huge amount of training to make it inside without tripping over one another," said Martha. She was a definite nerd when it came to tactics and loved to pick up information when she met frontline teams.

"You're right about the training," said Walker. "But you look as though you can handle yourself. And I must admit I have heard a bit about you — impressive. If you want to go down this line, just get in touch with me. I'll see you right."

"Thank you. I actually have considered this type of work but, ideally, I'd like to work in the anti-terror unit. But I guess they need firearms so maybe it could all work for the best."

Before she could say more, Walker said, "Flashbangs."

Martha looked at him.

"We use Flashbangs. A couple of those in an enclosed area and most people will be shaken and stirred as well as being deafened and dazzled."

Deciding to quit while she was ahead, Martha went back to her desk. Still nothing, but if Harry was right about the timings, there was possibly an hour to wait.

Time sped up as they headed towards the deadline. Martha had her phone on the desk so she wouldn't miss any calls. It was almost half an hour later when it beeped. As she called up the message, the Commander walked over.

Plans show there is a second basement not included in the official documents. Maybe more imminently.

He read it over her shoulder and almost ran back to his desk, ordering the same woman as earlier to get the strike team on line. The man leading the ground team listened quietly as the message was read out, asked for the words "second floor" to be repeated, and then was gone.

"He's a man of few words but brilliant at what he does," Walker said to Martha. "If nothing else, he'll be glad to be warned that people might appear from some hidden area. You really do not want to get in a fight in an enclosed space and one that may very well be in darkness.

"Anyway, not long now until the team goes in. I just hope that we get Tony Green — and maybe some of his henchmen too. I hate what he's done to the reputation of the Met. Even my strike teams — men and women who risk their lives for other people — get dragged down by it."

Looking at him, Martha thought he passionately believed in what he did. She also realised he was the first senior police officer she had spoken to in quite a while whom she felt she could completely trust.

"Five minutes," the voice of the woman who was working alongside Walker rang out.

Everyone paid more attention.

"Well, this is it, Martha. Don't hesitate to interrupt me if you get any information from now on. You will not be disturbing me."

"Thirty seconds."

Martha looked at the main screen. Still no activity at the door.

"Ten seconds."

Still nothing seemed to be happening.

"Five, four, three . . ."

Suddenly black-clad figures stormed the front door, seeming to flow through without stopping.

Flashbangs detonated and a voice came through.

"Level one clear."

Now the sound of the Flashbangs was muffled.

"Level two is clear."

The video feed from the helmet cameras worn by the assault team was difficult to follow. It started to settle down as the team leader came on.

"That feels like it was too easy. No opposition or even signs of life and both levels were open."

Martha's phone pinged. Walker swung round.

She read the message and shouted at him, "There's a third level."

Walker grabbed the microphone and bellowed, "It's a trap. There's a third level. Get out. It's a trap."

CHAPTER 62

Bullets ripped into the assault team as the criminals opened up. A Flashbang detonated, adding blinding flashes of light and bone-rattling noise to the hellish mix. It could have been a massacre as Green's team claimed the advantage of preparation.

But Walker's team were well trained and prepared. With bullets flying in their direction, they began a rapid withdrawal, so fast that a semi-conscious man was dragged out of the firing line by his feet. His war was over seconds after it began.

Two sergeants were laying down a withering protective fire that forced Green's men to hold their positions. It was the covering fire that saved many lives as not only did it prevent Green's mob from getting into position where they could return fire, it also allowed Walker's team to slowly withdraw from the kill zone.

Walker had been looking on in horror. He had barely moved, barely breathed since bellowing his warning at his soldiers. Now he waited a little longer as he saw his troops were safely out of firing range. All were taking the chance to reload.

The team leader's voice came over the comms. "Withdrawing to safe zone after my order. Protection team check we have all survivors. Countdown starts now. Three. Two. One . . . GO."

To his frustration, the comms unit played up and he lost sound.

"Assault Team Two. Can you hear me?"

"Affirmative."

"You're to go in as soon as you feel ready. Be warned, we've lost all contact with Team One so assume they don't know you are coming in. I do not want our people killed by friendly fire. We also now know there is a third level so proceed with the utmost caution. You need to secure that third floor. Do you have any questions?"

"No questions and clearly understood. We are ready to go and will enter in ten seconds from now."

The second team moved steadily through the building.

"First level checked. All clear. There is a staircase going down to the second level. There is an overwhelming smell of gunpowder and I am now hearing voices."

The camera feeds showed the descent and they could all hear the sounds of men in pain, calling out for assistance.

"We're checking the wounded now. A third staircase leads down. We will not descend until we have control of the situation here. I will report in shortly."

There was a long wait then the Team Two leader was back on.

"We have four of our people dead. Two critically injured and four less badly wounded but still in need of urgent attention. One of the men says they were trapped when a wall slid down and they were fired upon.

"This is starting to feel like a booby trap. I suggest the best thing to do is stay here, ensure the wounded are protected and only then approach level three. Do you agree?"

"Affirmative. I don't want to lose another team member," said Commander Walker.

"I have a question, sir," came the voice of the Team Two leader. "If this does turn out to have been a massive setup, do we have any idea who did that?"

"We have a few people in mind," said Walker.

Martha, who was looking on, didn't like the look he gave her but was careful not to show it. This was not a time to raise your head over the parapet, not with four people lying dead and maybe more before the day was out. As far as she could tell, this had all the hallmarks of Tony Green. Hidden levels, ambushes and that twisted cleverness of his that had managed to set the whole thing up. Unfortunately, it put Martha, Harry, Julie and Justin firmly in the frame. Green had turned them all into useful idiots. She should have been more sceptical.

Suddenly, her hand flew to her mouth and she felt like she'd been punched in the chest. The horrific failure of the assault team had pushed every other thought from her mind . . . including the safety of Betty. Her thoughts ran riot as she imagined what might be happening back at her home.

She called Harry and almost shouted with relief when he answered straight away. "Is everything okay?" It was short but the best she could manage.

"Nothing to worry about here. Everything is in place to make sure it stays that way. Just as we talked about."

"Thank God. I'll tell you more when I get home but things have gone badly south here so I'm not sure when I will be allowed to go. Until I do get out, you are in charge."

Walker was staring at her, his impatience clear.

"I need to go," said Martha. "I don't think I will be able to tell you anything more than you already know. What I can do is to give you all I have been able to unearth about this."

Walker continued to glare but finally backed down. Martha sensed a sliding doors moment. One way took her to fame and glory, the other to total humiliation and the end of her career and reputation.

The way he was still looking at her made Martha think he was giving serious thought to having her arrested. She felt he had a case, a pretty good one.

"Don't forget your phone," he said.

She took it as a dismissal and headed out. Walking to the tube station, she heard the sirens of the emergency services growing in volume until they merged into a distress call as they got closer and closer to the mansion.

But as fast as they got there it was already too late for some.

CHAPTER 63

By the time Martha got back, her home was in chaos. As she shut the front door behind her, she was hit with a bundle of joy and energy otherwise known as her daughter. Betty was home and was loving it.

"Isn't it great? We've got Harry's homemade chips for tea and special chocolate cake for pudding. I can have ice cream as well and Julie says she wants ice cream too."

Despite the fact her daughter was talking at about ten words a second, Martha could make out what she was saying. Then the words suddenly morphed into squeals of laughter as she shot up in the air, before spinning upside down, held by an ankle.

"Put me down, Julie! I am the Princess of Dulwich and you must do as I say."

"But I heard you giving away my ice cream secret. Now you must use the magic words or I put you in the dustbin."

More squeals, then Betty said, "Please put me down, Julie."

"I cannot resist. I will put you on the ground." Julie spun the little girl round again so that she landed on her feet.

"I need to do my homework before dinner — see you later!" Betty shot up the stairs.

The two women watched her run off to her room. Oblivious to the mounting danger around them, she was full of happiness. *If only*, thought Martha as she noticed Julie pointing up.

"Harry's fitted a new top bolt. We don't want Betty answering the door."

"Good idea."

"Come on down to the kitchen and tell us what happened. We've been watching the news, it sounds like the operation went terribly wrong."

Everyone was looking at the small TV on the back wall. It was showing the BBC News and the rolling headline at the foot of the screen said, *Five police officers killed and two critical after raid in London.*

A reporter was on camera on the main screen talking into his microphone. He pointed at a building some distance away. The camera zoomed in on a white stucco property with ambulances crowded outside. Two men in bright yellow high-vis clothes walked out of the front door with a stretcher. From this distance, the person on the stretcher appeared to be totally covered by a blanket.

"The police are holding us well back from the scene," said the reporter. "Until that stretcher was brought out, we had seen no one coming in or going out. We are being told that this was the scene of an armed police operation carried out in the rush hour.

"We have no information about this operation but we are told that four officers have died at the scene and two more are critical, having already been taken to hospital. Police say this is a major incident which remains ongoing and are investigating terrorism leaks.

"This is already a dark day for the Met and it could get worse. We understand that the families of all those involved today have been contacted. We will keep you informed of events as information about this terrible tragedy is released."

Harry reached up and turned the sound down. Martha gathered her thoughts.

"It was a setup. It has to be Green," she said. "It all started well then turned into hell just as you told us about the third level, Harry. Commander Walker tried to pull them back but it was too late. The survivors said a wall slid down and they were hit by automatic weapons fire.

"It was all so sudden that the police team didn't manage to get a shot off. They sent the backup unit in but the enemy was gone. They must have escaped through the lower level, although no one had any idea how that happened, at least not while I was still there.

"I watched the whole thing live. It was truly horrible and shocking. It only seemed to last a very short while then it was over and they were dead or wounded. I have never felt so frustrated, being miles away and nothing I could do to help."

Justin stood up and gave her a gentle hug. "Don't underestimate survival. You made it back, which means you can help get that bastard Green."

She hugged him back, grateful for the human touch and the reassurance of his words. But she knew it would be some time before she got over seeing the massacre.

Harry was busy handing round the tea. "I know you don't touch sugar normally, Martha, but I've put a spoon in your mug. Just this once. Drink it down. It will warm you up and make you feel better."

She did as instructed, almost gagging at the taste of the sweetness but, trusting Harry's instincts, she finished it off. Sure enough, a couple of minutes later, she was feeling less shaky and her racing thoughts slowed down.

It was Julie who asked the question that was on all of their minds. "What do you think will happen next? Do we need to bring in more people?"

"I don't think anything will happen tonight."

Martha's answer clearly surprised everyone so she carried on.

"For a start, every cop in London is going to be on full alert. Even some of those who are off duty will end up coming to work. Doing anything tonight would be very foolish with anyone calling 999 amazed at how fast the response is.

"Tony Green is many things, but foolish ain't one of them. He was an insider for years so he gets how it works. Tonight will be all about the reaction. Every copper in the Met is going to be thinking the same thing — move as fast as you can and you will get these people."

As she spoke, the TV pictures showed another covered stretcher coming out. She pointed at the screen. "Every serving officer, their partners, mothers, children, brothers and friends will be looking at that and thinking it could have been them, waving goodbye to their families this morning and never coming home. That's why the backlash will come tonight, while it's all fresh in the mind. Anyone involved in that will be mad if they don't just lie low."

She looked at Harry and saw that the scepticism of a few minutes ago was fading.

Martha pressed on. "Then there's Green himself. Setting up that trap at the house must have taken him a lot of thought and detailed planning. And he will have been hoping to grab one of us, preferably me.

"I can't see how he could manage to set up two operations on the same day. He would need the same planning time and the same manpower to set up a second attack like that. My guess is it's impractical. That doesn't mean we let our hair down, definitely not. But my gut says it's tomorrow when he makes his move. By then he will know — for sure — none of us was caught.

"In fact, don't take this the wrong way, but from what Harry's been told, you lot will just be a little bonus for him. It's me he wants. I say let him try. He won't like what happens when he does."

"I can hear your dad talking there, very clearly," said Harry. "He would never get involved in more than one thing at a time." He was carefully drying the frying pan for Betty's eggs and had one eye on the chip fryer, which was ready for cooking.

"I think you make a good point about Green, though. The one thing we do know about the man is that he creates elaborate plans. He's not just going to rush in to something. I'm a bit surprised he set this up at all. Let's be realistic, he can't have seriously expected that he would catch you since the chance of you being there would be almost non-existent. Think about it — most of the Met would be unlikely to let you hold a biro, let alone a gun."

"Exactly," said Martha. "If somewhat graphically put. There was never the slightest chance they would invite me to be part of that raid. I have the strongest sense he had no expectation of catching me in that house. So why put so much into it?"

The silence might have gone on if Betty hadn't turned up to announce she had one last thing to do in her homework and that she was ready to eat. Harry didn't need any more prompting.

"Five minutes and dinner is on the table." Betty left faster than she had arrived.

Martha couldn't help smiling at her daughter's innocent energy. It was worth being here just to see her smile. She jumped as her phone rang.

"Martha. It's Commander Walker. We need to talk, but I don't want it too official. How about you get to the barracks at 7 a.m. sharp tomorrow."

"Fine. See you then." Martha sounded considerably more confident than she felt.

"Good news?" said Justin using a tone that suggested he suspected otherwise.

"I wish I could say yes," she said, then ran everyone through the conversation. "What do you think?" she asked when she had finished.

It was Harry who spoke first. "They've just had a big operation blow up on them and now they're the filling in the sandwich with the top brass putting pressure on from above and the rank and file pushing from below demanding answers."

"Anyone got any bright ideas about my meeting with Walker?" Martha asked. "He seems to be about the straightest guy I've bumped into. I wish one of you could have been there. I'd have loved a second opinion."

"Apart from you need to get an early night, no," said Julie.

"That's not a bad idea. A plate of Harry's egg and chips, a hot bath then bed," said Martha. "But first, we have some planning to do."

CHAPTER 64

It was a dull, hot and oppressive day and the damp heat was making everyone miserable. Martha had opted for public transport, and even though it was just after 6 a.m., it felt oppressively tropical on the London Underground.

Deciding there was little point in hanging around, she made her way to the barracks. If they weren't ready for her, she could make use of the air conditioning inside the building to keep cool rather than suffer a low simmer waiting outside. On her previous visit, she'd thought the building was a touch on the cool side. She wouldn't be complaining this time.

Sitting down in the waiting area, she started reading the news on her phone but quickly switched it off. This didn't feel like the right place to be reading journalistic speculation. Not when she had played a key role in the tragedy.

At 6.45 a.m., the Commander walked in. He nodded at her then walked out. She quickly did the same. This time they ended up in an area that appeared to be for office or administrative functions. At the end of the corridor, Walker opened a door and Martha followed.

She was surprised at what she saw. It was a small room but comfortably furnished with a couple of armchairs in front of a desk, behind which was a leather office chair. Apart from the usual picture of the monarch, this one had several paintings, mostly the efforts of young children, and a couple of decent floral prints.

They sat in silence with neither attempting to make small talk.

"It's going to be seven all told," said Walker. "We're not making it public yet but the seventh victim is only being kept alive by machines. We're waiting for his brother to fly in from South America. We offered to do the formal stuff on his behalf but he insisted. He and his brother lost their parents when they were children so this stuff really matters.

"I brought you here because, while this is not exactly official, I've got you down as assisting inquiries. Better than heading off to a police station and making a statement."

"Are you looking to arrest me on the basis of something I say or don't say?" asked Martha.

"No. Not unless you confess." He looked sincere as he spoke and Martha judged that he meant what he said.

"Sorry to ask, but I would need to let people know if I was being held. I'd need to make arrangements for looking after my daughter. And don't get me wrong, but previous experience of being questioned makes me think getting a lawyer might be a good idea."

"I understand," said Walker. "You're good for the time being — that's the best I can tell you. Now, yesterday you couldn't let me have any more information about your source. Are you still taking the same position?"

Martha reached down and picked up her handbag from the floor. She placed it on the desk and pointed at it. "May I?"

He waved to indicate she could press ahead.

She pulled out a small envelope, inside which was a piece of card. She handed this to Walker. "This is the man — if you can find him. His name is Del Williams. He dropped out of sight very suddenly, just a few days ago. Not exactly a surprise as he does go AWOL from time to time. I was informed that he had been acting a little strangely.

"He's a bent copper, who's served time and kept some other coppers out of trouble, some of them very senior policemen six years ago and even more important now. As a result, there's a lot of people who owe him big time. To put it another way, he's about as well protected as you can get, especially since he's let it be known that he's left a list of names in the event something does happen to him. All in all, he's not the easiest man to find if he decides to vanish, especially with the favours he can call upon. Just in case it helps, I'm told that Albania and Bulgaria are considered the places he'd head to."

Walker looked at the name carefully handwritten in capitals. "You certainly mix with some interesting people."

"If there's one thing I have learned, it's that the world is a complicated place." Martha braced in case he wanted to make any more of it but he nodded to himself as he leaned forward and pressed a button on his desk phone.

Seconds later, a smartly dressed sergeant walked in. Walker handed him the paper. "That man knows more. He may be on the run, ex-Yard, served time."

The sergeant walked out.

Martha was impressed at the speed with which the information had been passed on and received.

"You run a tight ship here," she said.

"We have a sort of unofficial motto — one of several, actually — which says, 'Never use one word unless you have to.'"

The comment made her laugh. "I have a friend who says pretty much the same thing. He reckons that just because there's a silence, doesn't mean you have to fill it."

"I take it that would be Harry . . . Harry the hat? Used to be your dad's right-hand man and since his death he has become a sort of godfather to you. I also hear that he is remarkably fit, more than capable of mixing in with people half his age."

She really hadn't been expecting that answer. To her dismay, her mouth had dropped open in surprise.

"How—" She stopped herself completing the question. However he knew about Harry he wasn't going to be telling her.

So it came as an even bigger surprise when he said, "I used to know Harry quite well. He helped clear up a nasty little paedophile gang. I never found out where he got the information from but I came home one day to find him sitting outside. He had a very detailed dossier with him, all the names, addresses, victims and a load of pictures that made us both sick to look at but very pleased when a dozen of the bastards went down for life because of that evidence.

"Working on that, we discovered we were quite similar and went out for the odd drink or two. It was about eighteen years ago, about when you were running about in shorts . . . you never took to skirts, I was told, which made the arrests all the more poignant.

"A couple of years later, I took over a department that has never officially existed, so we lost touch. I wasn't allowed to speak to anyone from my old life. That was a shame because we had become mates.

"But it's a funny world that people like you and me live in. Full of shadows and dangerous people and never really knowing who you can talk to. And then, out of the blue, a connection is made or a door opens that leads you back to a friend you know you can trust."

To say Martha was taken aback would be an understatement. She was gobsmacked. "I don't mean to be blunt, but does this have something to do with today? I mean, I know it does but are you going to confirm that?"

"Yes," said Walker. "And I have been talking in riddles. The point is, I know that you didn't set up the ambush. And the reason I know that is because I discovered yesterday about your link to Harry. I mean, your name alone would have done it. Sorry if you haven't heard this before, but your dad was a bit marmite with most officers. I was firmly with the people who loved him. But when Harry vouched for you, I was convinced. I spoke to him briefly last night and he told me you are the bravest and most honest copper he has ever known. You'd sooner shoot yourself than do something criminal. That was enough for me."

"Okay," said Martha. "Let's say I go along with this — why didn't Harry let me know he had spoken to you?"

"He told me you'd bring that up. He said you'd probably be quite cross and I can tell from your expression that he was right."

Seeing she was about to speak, he went on. "We agreed to keep it from you, at least until now, because we felt it made you safer. We thought that if you knew you were in the clear, you might have looked more relaxed. When you arrived this morning, I was watching on CCTV and you looked like a woman with the troubles of the world on her mind. No one seeing you would have imagined you were anything other than deeply worried.

"Harry took the view that you should assume you were probably under surveillance and act accordingly. He was going to tell you last night but then changed his mind. He told me that anyone watching you would be convinced by how troubled you looked."

He stopped and raised a questioning eyebrow.

She responded with a deep sigh. "Believe it or not, I get it, even if it is a bit mad — no, make that very mad. I suppose this helps keep the other side in the dark and that can only help. I guess while I'm waiting, I can work on my anxiety. I need to develop it from this morning so that I can convince any watcher that I have received really bad news.

"Talking of how long before I can leave, it would be good if I can get back for lunch. I'm desperate to make sure my daughter doesn't pick up on what's going on."

"That sounds sensible. Shall we say you stay here until 11 a.m.?" Walker fixed his gaze straight on her. "But I do have some other news for you. News that you will find disturbing."

CHAPTER 65

Martha sat up straighter. "I seem to be hearing a lot of disturbing things recently. Must be that black cat I saw last week. What is it this time?" she asked.

"I'm going to tell it to you straight. You are the victim of a social media campaign that is spreading lies about you," said Walker. "Someone is trying to turn you into a pariah within police circles. And this campaign isn't one of those little amateurish jobs — it's sneaky, plausible and nasty."

"I don't understand," said Martha. "How can someone be doing that? And I take it we are probably talking about Tony Green here. Surely no one can take that man seriously anymore."

Walker steepled his fingers. "It's one thing knowing in your heart it's Tony Green, it's quite another to prove it. And he's far too careful to have his fingerprints anywhere near it.

"This is being done in a very relentless fashion and it is getting through to police officers — and not just the rank and file. Normally with these things most of the messages are left on sites that provide very high levels of encryption. Unless you've been sent the message directly, you will never know about it. But this time someone is spreading rumours out in the open."

"So what are they saying about me?" demanded Martha.

Walker pulled a face. He hated this sort of character assassination where the accuser remained hidden and the victim didn't have a chance to defend themselves properly. It was a particular source of frustration that so many police officers were taken in by it. If anyone should know better, it was a copper.

"I'm afraid it is being claimed that you are responsible for what happened last night. Police officers are being told that you set the whole thing up and had been planning this for years.

"Earlier on, you talked about something being a bit mad. Well this is batshit crazy. The suggestion is that you are looking to get revenge on your father's enemies . . . and now it gets totally weird. I have seen one post that says you tried to involve the sons and daughters of police officers who were exposed by your father. Quite mad."

Martha wasn't having to fake the look of consternation on her face. "That couldn't be any further from the truth. How can anyone believe this sort of nonsense?"

"I agree with you," said Walker. "The trouble is that some people seem to take a deliberate delight in spreading this sort of material. Officers like yourself, ones with a high profile, are often targeted. Then you get the 'no smoke without fire' mob. They're always keen to make mischief. And you also have some serious enemies, people who want to do you harm.

"What worries me is if this gets out from police circles — maybe to the media. If they get their hands on this, who knows where it will end? People lose all ability to be sceptical about what they're reading. And it gets passed on with such speed that the sensible voices get drowned out."

Martha didn't know whether to laugh or cry. "Is there anything of this that I can read?"

"By all means," said Walker. "Just so you know we are trying to get it backtracked but no luck so far. Whoever did this really knows what they're doing."

He gazed at her with a sombre expression.

"I'm beginning to recognise that look." Martha felt ice forming in her stomach.

"There's more and this is the worst."

"Go on," she said.

At first he said nothing, then reached for a glass of water, which he gulped down.

"There's talk of a bounty being put on your head."

CHAPTER 66

Martha was so shocked she barely remembered the journey home, and had no recollection of leaving Walker. When she came in, Harry, Julie and Justin were so alarmed by her appearance they had her sitting down within seconds. Then they all fired questions at her as she waved frantically, asking them to slow down.

It was Justin who calmed things down. "Come on, guys, we need to give her some space. I think we're all just making things worse. Why don't we take it more slowly?"

He rested his hand lightly on her shoulder. "Sorry about that, but if you don't mind me saying so, you look like you've seen a ghost. Can you tell us what's wrong? Or maybe you need a cup of Harry's tea?"

"Tea sounds fabulous," said Martha. "And sorry if I've worried you, but I will be fine in a minute. It might be an idea if we all had a cup then I can tell you."

Making sure to leave nothing out, she ran through everything that had happened — it had been an eventful morning. When she got to the part about Harry and Walker talking together, Julie gave her sparring partner a long stare. For his part he looked abashed.

"For a moment, just after you arrived back home," he said, "I did wonder if not telling you about Walker had given you a far too big a shock. But then I reminded myself that you are one of the toughest people around and it wouldn't have bothered you to that extent . . . I hope I'm right about that." He looked like a man who was starting to wish he hadn't done something and was now casting around for a plausible explanation.

"You are, Harry," said Martha. "It was nothing you did. What troubled me was a very unpleasant introduction to the world of social media and finding myself not just getting criticised for my hair colour, but far worse, my professionalism — and finding out that there was a bounty on my head."

She talked them through what she had seen in Walker's office and when she got to the threats against Betty, Julie picked up the iPad and waved it furiously in front of her. "You mean one of these stupid things is allowing cowards to make threats without having to say who they are? Well, I tell you what, I'm going to find these people then let's see how tough they are when they've had their arms ripped off." She gave the iPad an extra strong shake then stared at it as if she might tear it into pieces with her bare hands.

"It might be best if you gave that to me," said Harry, who suspected Julie could inflict some serious damage to the device if she was left to it. He held out his hand and waited for her to pass it over. Trying to force it out of her massive fists would be as pointless as using a teaspoon to empty a bath.

Martha watched the exchange between the pair and gave thanks that she had two such loyal friends in her life. She had been badly shaken up when Commander Walker showed her the online material calling for her death. Most sickening was the threat against Betty. Reading it had sent cold shivers down her spine followed by an intense feeling of nausea.

Justin who was, by common acclaim, the internet guru, said, "I think I know where this is going. I expect that what you'd like to know, at least to kick off with, is, can we track down the people responsible and stop them?"

No one interrupted so he carried on.

"The first thing to say, Martha, is you are not the first person to have had such a horrible thing happen to you, so don't go blaming yourself or tolerating that other great invention, victim blaming. You didn't do this and the people who did are wicked.

"As Julie said, and it's one of the worst things about the web, it's a favourite hiding place for bullies and cowards who don't have the guts to say anything in public."

"Thank you for that, Justin. I must admit that just being here with you guys has helped me no end. I think it was reading about Betty that temporarily scrambled my brains. I used to think people who got upset about personal attacks on social media were getting everything out of proportion . . . never again! This stuff is evil, there's no other word for it."

"You're right there," said Justin. "So I guess the big question is, what can we do about it? I'm afraid the answer is not as much as we might wish. A lot of people who post this sort of stuff do make some effort to disguise themselves. It isn't that hard for them but makes it harder for us.

"If you go down the path of tracking people down it can be time-consuming and very confusing. By the time you've managed to reverse out of every blind alley you've been sent down, it can be very dispiriting."

"Sorry to interrupt, but couldn't we just stop the platforms carrying this stuff?" asked Martha. "That would take us to the heart of the problem."

"That's what you might think," said Justin. "But it's quite difficult in reality. I expect you think I'm just coming up with excuses . . . Let me explain. Let's say you want to ring Facebook, what number do you call?"

There were blank looks and shrugs all round.

Justin looked back at them. "Like I said, it's not easy. There is a way that helps — do you have an important friend who just happens to have Facebook on speed dial? If you do, great. But even then, there's still a lot to do.

"You need them to take down every reference to it, but by now the post's been up for a while and has spread so it's got to be found. And you're not the only people who need stuff taken down. You can see why it gets tricky.

"To be honest, the real problem is that the internet is a cesspit and contains the vilest things you can imagine."

"Is what you're really saying is that we have no chance?" asked Martha.

"Never give up. You taught me that, Martha. I'm just saying don't hold your breath."

The kitchen fell silent for a moment. Not even Julie, who was the most optimistic person anyone knew, could think of anything to say.

When Harry's phone rang they all jumped, including Harry.

He picked up. The caller had such a strong South London accent that even though they could all hear him clearly on loudspeaker, they couldn't understand a word.

Harry listened intently. "Are you certain it's the cops?"

The voice said something in an angry tone, which seemed to include the words, "I can smell the filth."

There was another incomprehensible exchange then the connection was cut.

"I think we may be in trouble. The cops have turned up out of the blue and are taking pictures of all our people outside. They've never been interested in us at all — up to now. I guess your thought that every police officer would want to be on the case is happening already."

"That's a little bit quicker than I might have hoped. Let's see if we can find out exactly what's going on," said Martha. "Did they say which unit they are from? If we can get a name, I might be able to enlist the Commissioner and get them to back off."

"That's just it," said Harry, who was already on another phone call. "The people hassling our people won't say who they are but my bloke says there is no question they are cops. They're acting like cops, totally full of themselves and not interested in what we have to say. They're all armed and don't give a toss about what happens to us if our guards are chased off."

Harry listened again then turned to Martha. "He wants to talk to you, shall I put him on speaker?"

She threw him a questioning look.

"He's one of our best men and has been looking out for you since this all started."

He sounded perfect. Martha flashed Harry a thumbs up.

"Hi, Martha. Eddie here. I'd better be quick, but I wanted to let you know we're there for you. And I wanted to tell you that once we've gone, there's a moment that might work in our favour.

"At some point very soon you will be told you are being taken away from the house. Before that, the Old Bill will run into problems with their cars. Actually, it's just a small problem but that is where you might get a chance to escape. You'll have to judge everything in the moment, I'm afraid.

"I'll slow things down as much as I can but they're warning us that we'll be cuffed and taken away. I can escalate this. Most of my blokes will join me. Just say the word and we can get a few involved, maybe give you a chance to run for it, because I think we all know who's coming next."

"No, Eddie, you're not to take risks. I will not have someone get hurt out there. And don't think I'm not grateful to you."

"If you're sure, Martha."

Martha ended the call and folded her arms. She looked as angry as anyone had seen her before.

"If those bastards think they can push us around, then they are making a mistake of underestimating us. Well, let's show them what we can do if we put our minds to it."

Her short rallying cry inspired Julie, who punched Justin painfully in the arm, making it feel numb. He hoped he recovered quickly — he would never live it down if he failed to make the first hurdle, especially carrying an injury inflicted by one of his own side.

Fortunately, the sensation was slowly returning to his limb and he flexed his tingling fingers cautiously. All five digits responded, so he took that as a good sign.

"What do you all think about me calling Paula Charteris?" said Martha. "She might be able to do something."

"If it suits her and she actually wants to," said Julie, who had lost all faith in the Commissioner. Not that she'd had much to lose in the first instance.

"To be honest, Martha," said Harry, "I think we have to treat her as one of the enemy. I mean, by all means call her, but I bet you can't get through to her and then even if she did offer to help, could we trust her?"

Martha looked around. "Okay, we'll forget about the Commissioner for now. Harry, you heard the conversation just now. There's no outside help coming. It's just us. What is the current state of play outside?"

Harry was talking to yet another person. He passed on Martha's question and listened to the reply.

His eyes brows shot up. "Someone is throwing the kitchen sink at us."

CHAPTER 67

Martha checked the time — just after 1 p.m. It was time to move and she needed to be quick.

She glanced around and was relieved to see Harry talking on the phone in an animated way. He would be cross that she was leaving without telling him what she was up to.

She jutted her chin. She'd been over this many times and on this occasion it was best to leave him out of the loop. The trouble was that everyone knew him. In some circles, Harry had near celebrity status, especially among the criminal fraternity. Which meant that rather more people would be looking at him and not her.

And not being looked at was very useful. It meant that she had a tiny bit of freedom that could be exploited without drawing attention and it was almost time to do just that.

Martha took her opportunity and slipped out of the room. She didn't need long. There aren't many places to go in a small house and this one was no different. She sighed.

The downstairs toilet was towards the back of the house. Martha quickly walked in and shut the door behind her. She checked the seat and sat down, recalling the part of the conversation she'd had with Commander Walker on leaving him at the barracks that morning.

"I'm worried. I'm utterly convinced something is going to happen to my people. I think I need to try and arrange protection for us, but this has to be kept secret."

The Commander didn't skip a beat. "I totally agree with you, especially with what is happening on social media. Harry has told me about your antennae for trouble. We have a firearms squad rotating back into the work diary. No one knows they are back yet so they can be our ace in the hole."

They wrapped up their conversation and Martha thanked Walker.

Sitting on the loo, Martha pressed 'send' to the message that she had quickly typed, then went to the front of the house. She was surprised at the amount of activity that was going on in the road.

"There must be a dozen police vehicles out there," she said when she returned to the kitchen. "They're picking up all our people then taking them away."

The activity forcefully brought home that they were edging closer to the showdown with Tony Green. Harry made a private vow to himself. If it came to it, he would willingly sacrifice his own life to save Martha and Betty and that might come tonight. They were packed inside a small Victorian house in Dulwich, South London. They literally had nowhere else to go.

The doorbell rang. Harry waved everyone to sit down except Julie, who he grabbed by the wrist. This way, he knew where she was so if anything kicked off he could indicate the hot points.

They opened the front door to be greeted by the sight of three armed men. The man in front appeared to be the leader and wasted no time on small talk. Over the years, Harry had spent time with a lot of ex-service people. These three were doing their best to come across as hard men, desperate to be thought of as SAS, but Harry knew better. You don't spend a chunk of your life mixing with Special Forces not to be able to spot the real thing. These three were not. They were fake.

Martha had stressed no guns, but Harry had eventually worn her down and got her to amend this stance. It was now no guns unless they fired first. Martha wasn't really happy about it — she couldn't bear the thought of Betty being involved or, even worse, shot — but she trusted Harry to make the right call, when it came.

Unaware of the conversation Harry was having in his head, the leader of the trio was striking a pose with his chest puffed out and arms folded.

"We need to check your house," he said. "And I mean now."

"Show me some ID," said Harry.

The leader gathered himself and produced a card, which he flashed around too fast to see and put back in his pocket.

Then he waved his gun. "This can go hard or it can go easy. Choose, Grandad."

Harry smiled one of his non-smiles but waved them inside. Walking into the kitchen, he pointed at the three. "These men claim to be police officers. They say they want to check your house, Martha."

Martha folded her arms. "I need to see some ID first and then you can explain yourselves."

"If you insist," said the leader, who was starting to regain his composure. He reached for his 'card' and quickly flashed it.

"Hey," said Martha. "Show me that again?"

"No more messing about," said the leader, all but sneering. He was a big, well-muscled man and clearly felt confident handling himself. He'd also managed to convince himself that he hadn't just been stared out by a pensioner.

Martha glanced at her friends. She knew they would hold their own in a fight but the enemy was armed and it only took a moment to fire a gun. She signalled them to stand down by making a pressing motion with her palm facing down.

"Good decision," said the leader. "We're here to check on the welfare of a little girl, Betty. Your daughter, Martha, if I'm not mistaken?"

A shocked silence fell and Harry was showing signs of moving when the leader added, "I have a social services team outside. One of you can go and check if you like."

Martha felt the need to try and exert some control, urgently. "Justin, can you go? It makes sense, you being her dad."

He stood up and left straight away. Julie looked on with a deep frown. Martha knew she was worried that they were getting separated.

"I think it's the best idea for now," said Martha.

Justin was back sooner than she expected but she was in a mental place where the passage of time was playing tricks. Justin could have been gone five minutes or fifteen minutes.

"They are here, just waiting down the road. They showed me ID that is the sort of thing I have seen before and they looked the part. They have been told there is an urgent need to get Betty out of the area."

Martha felt like her back was to the wall and wasn't quite sure which way to turn.

"Okay." Martha made a choice. "Justin, you get Betty and make sure she packs clothes, schoolwork and whatever she needs for a few days. I think it's the best decision as it keeps her safe."

As she spoke, she was eyeballing Harry and Julie. They weren't impressed but they would do as she said.

Betty appeared from upstairs looking scared but determined. Martha's heart went out to her. She was being so brave. Justin must have managed to think of something to say. She ran to Martha and held her in a big hug.

"Daddy says you both want me to go. I'd rather stay here. Can I?"

"I'm sorry, angel, but Daddy is right," said Martha. "The grown-ups need to talk and you will be better off with Daddy."

Justin appeared with a bag and the same expression as Betty. But, like her, he was willing to follow directions from Martha. As Betty looked back at them, Martha thought her heart might swell to bursting with pride.

"I've got everything, as you said. I can go with her—"

Justin got no further as one of the alleged cops smashed him hard on the back of the head. He dropped instantly, like a bag of flour, blood gushing from the wound.

Betty dropped to her knees and screamed — a sound Martha would never forget — and then stopped. A stocky woman had sneaked in, grabbed the little girl, and was holding her tightly by the wrist. Her daughter tried to fight back but it was no contest. The woman was strong and expert at her job. It only took seconds for Betty to be marched out of the house.

Martha was struggling to absorb what had happened. It was so fast yet Justin was down, and Betty had gone. She thought she had prepared for this moment — but not even close. This was beyond her worst nightmare.

Out of the corner of her eye, she sensed Harry was preparing to move. He was fast but Martha was faster. "No, Harry — they've got Betty."

Harry stopped in his tracks as he absorbed what Martha had said. His eyes widened as reality barged in.

There was a deafening bang. Someone had fired a gun.

CHAPTER 68

Martha stood in the kitchen that she had known all her life. Instead of warm laughter and the smell of freshly brewed tea, she was now enveloped by the tang of gun smoke and the distinctive metallic odour of blood. The horror she surveyed was that of her two wonderful friends lying on the floor with blood oozing from their wounds.

She had watched Harry be thrown backwards, banging his head before landing heavily on his back. Blood was slowly spreading across the kitchen floor. His eyes were shut and he had gone grey. Martha resisted moving over to him as she had a gun pointing straight at her.

Lucy stood in the doorway holding the weapon. She was the one who was now in control. Julie was wounded but her pride had taken a bigger hit. "You fucking bitch! You just shot me!"

"I would put another one in you but there are going to be some very unpleasant things done to you later on, so I'll enjoy watching that later . . . Now, shut up!"

Martha caught Julie's eye and in their silent exchange, Martha said, *Just keep quiet for now.*

In the background, she could hear sirens. She sincerely hoped they were coming here, it was the best she'd been able to arrange at short notice. All she could do was hope. The wailing grew in volume but still no one reacted. The noise was part of the background in London and could be heard day and night.

She glanced down again and this time she made herself look. Two of the people she loved most in the world were lying on her kitchen floor injured, maybe dying if they didn't get that blood loss under control. Her beautiful daughter — who she did love the most — had been snatched. It was an awful word, snatched. Who went around telling people they were snatchers? There were so many bad-sounding words. Grabbed, seized, kidnapped. You wouldn't want to hang around with anyone who did that either.

Martha blinked and took a deep breath. Slow down, girl, and stop playing daft word games. It was not going to help. She could see that Harry was recovering from the shock of being shot. He had colour in his face again, not the grey tinged with green from a few moments ago. Martha thanked the stars that he was a seemingly indestructible old git as he was looking defiantly at Lucy.

"Don't even think about it, Harry," said Lucy. "It's not the time to be a hero."

Harry sneered. "You will never know safety again. You can kill me, kill Julie, kill Justin, kill Martha . . . still people will come for you. You don't think I leave things to fate? I leave nothing to fate. Like I said, you will be ended in a way you deserve."

Lucy squirmed as the words hit home. These were not idle threats. She lived in a dog-eat-dog world and there was a code. Still, she had made her decision to get the payday of her life and disappear after this job, safely into retirement.

Martha could hear a commotion in the small hallway. The kitchen door opened and Tony Green sauntered in, looking around as though he was considering buying the house. She could hear Harry grind his teeth so hard she was surprised his jaw didn't crack.

"Don't be like that, Harry," said Green. "You of all people always knew this would come down to a gunfight. And you can't seriously believe any of you were going to walk away from here. Not after what you did to me. I simply will not be disrespected. By anyone."

He waved the gun in Harry and Julie's direction. "If you want to stop breathing, just try to move."

Green switched his attention to Martha, who was standing like a statue at the end of the kitchen table. "I'm going to have a lot of fun with you. I have a special room all set up so I can spend some quality time with you, making what's left of your life hell."

Martha tugged at her right ear. "Well, I doubt you will ever get the chance. Certainly not here, not ever."

Like a wounded lion, Harry let out a tremendous roar. Green turned. The noise badly unsettled him and he took his eye off everyone except Harry. It meant he missed Martha reaching under the kitchen table to pick up a pair of handguns taped there for just this sort of moment.

She had practised for this and it showed. In one fluid movement she had one of the guns in her right hand.

As luck would have it, Green was facing away. She stopped, lined up his head and fired. It was a classic double tap. One to kill. One to be certain.

Blood and brains splattered against the kitchen door. Martha went to line up Lucy, which was when the woman got lucky. In her panic to escape she trod on her feet and fell straight to the floor. Martha grunted as her quarry dropped like a stone.

As she looked around, the bloodlust faded. "Your lucky day," she told Lucy.

Martha was already on the move. She needed to find Betty.

As she ran for the front door, a succession of medics and troopers poured in. She shrank against the wall as they barged past. Three more people raced in then Martha headed out.

The sun was shining in so it was difficult to see, and her heart was pounding. Betty was right there, disguised by the sharp sunlight.

In the midst of this, Justin found Martha and Betty. He was looking groggy but was more on the walking-wounded end of the spectrum.

Justin wrapped his arms around Martha and Betty and held them tightly. "I'm so pleased you are both safe," he said through tears.

Most people had drifted away but there was a handful of the clean-up crew working at removing blood spatter and grabbing fingerprints and photos.

One of the team walked over. "I'm looking for Martha."

"You've found her."

"Great. This is for you." She handed her a leatherbound book that she guessed was a diary.

"It was found in a false pocket in Tony Green's trousers," said the woman. She walked away.

"Are you going to look at it, Martha?" asked Harry, who was clutching his shoulder and trying to fight off an overenthusiastic paramedic.

"Not tonight and I doubt there is anything consequential in it."

What she didn't add was that she knew what it was. And if that had surfaced, there was trouble ahead.

THE END

THE JOFFE BOOKS STORY

We began in 2014 when Jasper agreed to publish his mum's much-rejected romance novel and it became a bestseller.

Since then we've grown into the largest independent publisher in the UK. We're extremely proud to publish some of the very best writers in the world, including Joy Ellis, Faith Martin, Caro Ramsay, Helen Forrester, Simon Brett and Robert Goddard. Everyone at Joffe Books loves reading and we never forget that it all begins with the magic of an author telling a story.

We are proud to publish talented first-time authors, as well as established writers whose books we love introducing to a new generation of readers.

We won Trade Publisher of the Year at the Independent Publishing Awards in 2023 and Best Publisher Award in 2024 at the People's Book Prize. We have been shortlisted for Independent Publisher of the Year at the British Book Awards for the last five years, and were shortlisted for the Diversity and Inclusivity Award at the 2022 Independent Publishing Awards. In 2023 we were shortlisted for Publisher of the Year at the RNA Industry Awards, and in 2024 we were shortlisted at the CWA Daggers for the Best Crime and Mystery Publisher.

We built this company with your help, and we love to hear from you, so please email us about absolutely anything bookish at feedback@joffebooks.com.

If you want to receive free books every Friday and hear about all our new releases, join our mailing list here: www.joffebooks. com/freebooks.

And when you tell your friends about us, just remember: it's pronounced Joffe as in coffee or toffee!